A DEADLY AWAKENING

>   >   >

He was jolted from his sleep by an insistent jabbing at his ribs. Dazed and bewildered, Jud Hilliard came up on one elbow, and was held there by the demanding pressure of a gun muzzle boring against him.

"Far enough!" was the harsh order. "Stay that way!"

"Just who in hell do you think..." and before Hilliard had time to finish, he received a savage blow across the face.

"That enough answer for you...?"

Jud Hilliard's first surge of dazed and bewildered anger had been merely hot and resentful. Now it became a wild, raging fury. Flat on his back though he was on the bed, he doubled his knees and drove both booted feet at the leering face above him and sent the man floundering backward. Fast as a cat, Hilliard was up and after him, hammering a vengeful fist home that sent the man all the way down, slamming his head against the floor and jarring the gun from his hand.

Hilliard dove for it...

Also by L.P. Holmes

Payoff at Pawnee
Flame of Sunset
Brandon's Empire
Catch and Saddle
Night Marshal
Hill Smoke
The Plunderers
High Starlight

**Published by
WARNER BOOKS**

THE DISTANT VENGEANCE

L.P. HOLMES

WARNER BOOKS

A Warner Communications Company

WARNER BOOKS EDITION

Warner Books, Inc.
666 Fifth Avenue
New York, N.Y. 10103

A Warner Communications Company

Printed in the United States of America

First Printing: February, 1987

10 9 8 7 6 5 4 3 2 1

CHAPTER

1

UNDER the overhang of a deep, galleried porch the evening's warm dusk was layered so thickly that Jud Hilliard had to resort to the frugal light of a sulfur match to decipher the words written on the sheet of paper tacked to the building's locked door: CLOSED UNTIL FURTHER NOTICE. FOR PARTICULARS SEE JONATHAN PEABODY.

Sitting his saddle with the forward-leaning eagerness of a man returning home after long absence, Hilliard had ridden into Meridian on a towering, smooth-striding roan, his glance searching for well remembered and greatly treasured scenes.

1

All along the way streetlights appeared, spreading their radiance from doors and windows left open against the day's lingering heat. But no lights burned in this long, low building which stood halfway up street on the right-hand side. The lack of light struck sharply home with Hilliard, stirring up a biting concern. For in the days he so fervently recalled, Pop Worley's Longhorn Mercantile had always been the first place in town to open and the last to close, its lights burning early and late.

The store had supplied the community with many things, including mail service. By rights, at this time of the evening, the deep, hospitable porch should have been busy with ranchers from the vast, open range nearby, together with the usual gathering of town regulars, all eager to see Pop Worley empty the mail sack that arrived daily by stage from Haden Creek Junction. There also should have been several buckboards and spring wagons in the street out front, with a scatter of saddle stock tied along the lengthy hitch rail.

That was how it had been in the old days. But not now. On this warm and gentle evening the store building lay dark, the porch and street and hitch rail completely empty. When the dismal meaning of these facts registered, Hilliard had been swift to dismount, duck under the hitch rail, climb the low steps of the porch, and read the message on the door.

He read it a second time with a steadily mounting apprehension and became momentarily still, not discarding the match until its final spark scorched his fingers. Hilliard searched his memory to dredge up a nearly forgotten name. When he finally had it, he spoke it aloud.

"Jonathan Peabody! He was the banker...!"

Back on the street, Hilliard led his horse toward the center of town. Afoot, as in the saddle, he was a rangy man, carrying a pair of solid, well-packed shoulders with a balanced erectness that suggested a touch of military training. The bank, as he now recalled, stood across the street from the hotel. As he approached the bank he glimpsed a lamp glowing in a window beside the door. He tried the door but found it locked, so he rapped on it insistently. A stir of movement came presently, the lock clicked, and the door opened just wide enough to let out a blast of angry, irascible protest.

"All right—all right! Who is it and what the devil do you want? Don't you know it's way past banking hours, and because I happened to be working late—now this! Once more—who are you?"

Hilliard's answer was as terse as the greeting had been. "It's Hilliard, Mr. Peabody—Jud Hilliard, just arrived back home!"

The door quickly opened wide, spilling enough lamp glow to bring Hilliard into clear view. The banker stepped forward and stared, as though unable to believe his own eyes.

"Not—not Jud Hilliard! It can't be! The official report that reached us here in Meridian stated again and again that there were no survivors, that all with Custer were dead—wiped out. So this can't be Jud Hilliard...!"

"But it is, Mr. Peabody. I'm real enough," Hilliard assured him. He followed these words with a blunt demand. "That message on the store door—what does it mean? What about Pop? Where is he?"

Jonathan Peabody was spare-bodied and thin-faced, his head topped with an upstanding roach of gray hair. His bank was a one-man institution at which he often worked late, keeping his records in top shape, being careful and meticulous about such things. Now he scrubbed a hand across his face, then gripped Hilliard by the arm, as though seeking an assurance of reality by the contact. He steadied and spoke in a quieter tone.

"Come in, boy—come in! And don't think me a doddering old fool. We had only that one published report on the Bighorn affair to go by, and it seemed so definite and final! About Pop? He's gone, Jud. We buried the old fellow near four months ago. I wrote you at Fort Lincoln telling of his death. You never got my letter?"

Jud Hilliard did not answer immediately. Grimness deepened in him, and the last show of eagerness faded from his eyes, leaving him bleak. Only a shadow of hurt remained in the glance he gave the banker. He shook his head slowly.

"I got no letter. It was probably lost, along with so many other things that were lost in that disastrous campaign. When I finally got back to Lincoln, all that awaited me was my discharge, my enlistment having run out while I was in the field. They offered me a sergeancy if I'd sign on for another hitch, but I wasn't interested. I'd served my stint and wanted to get back to the freedom of civilian life. Now, once more about Pop. What took him off? Sickness of some sort or just the many, many years?"

Jonathan Peabody hesitated, as though reluctant to say what had to be said. "Neither, Jud. He was killed, shot to death in a late-night holdup."

Hilliard stiffened. Harshness pulled him up taut, and he towered above the little banker.

"Shot? In a holdup? Who by?"

Jonathan Peabody shrugged wearily. "No answer to that. So easy, boy—easy! There are things I can tell you and things I can't. We've considerable to talk over, you and me. We both miss old Pop. So does everybody in these parts. Nothing would please the folks round about more than to lay violent hands on Pop's killer and hang him from the nearest tree. But the killer is gone, nobody knows where, so we can't rush any answers. Personally, right now I'm ready to call it a day. I could stand a drink and something to eat. No doubt you could too. So let's go over to the hotel."

Jud Hilliard had steadied, no longer ravaged by the initial burst of raw anger and grief that had ripped through him. Now, too, in some strange way, the mounting sense of loss tended to quiet him. So he nodded slowly.

"Have to take care of my horse, first. There's still a working stable in town?"

"Hutch Baker's layout—stable and corrals," Peabody said. "Far end of the street. I'll wait for you in the hotel bar."

Once the big red horse was safely stabled for the night, Hilliard returned to find Jonathan Peabody standing at the hotel bar with bottle and glasses before him. The banker filled the glasses and lifted his. "To better days, Jud!"

"As if there could be any of such now," Hilliard answered bitterly.

Peabody drained his glass, put it back on the bar. "Pop wouldn't want you to feel that way, boy. He left you a better legacy. Now, how's about supper?"

They sat at a small side table in the dining room, and a middle-aged waitress brought their meal.

Hilliard waited until the waitress moved on before laying a demanding glance on the banker. "All right, tell it! About Pop. How did it happen?"

Peabody lifted a warding hand. "Presently, boy, presently. Give me time to straighten out my thinking, because it still bewilders me to look at you and know that you are real. That report on Custer sounded so damn final. No survivors, it said. All gone. And to me that meant you were gone too, because I knew you were in the Seventh Cavalry under Custer."

"Under him but not actually with him on that particular day," Hilliard said, correcting him. "My outfit was with Reno. Oh, we went up the valley of the Little Bighorn, all right, running into our share of rough treatment and leaving a number of good men there. But Custer was way out ahead of us, on the other side of the hill, reaching for glory and finding only disaster and death. Personally I had more than my share of luck, which is why I'm here tonight."

"How could it have happened, boy?" Peabody pressed. "All of it, I mean? Such a crushing, overwhelming defeat? What went wrong? What were the reasons?"

Hilliard shrugged. "There were a number. First of all, we ran into a lot more Sioux warriors than we expected. Also, there was never anything lacking in courage and fighting ability with those people. Beyond that, they were well armed not only with their native weapons of lance and bow and arrow, but also with repeating rifles that in such a battle were far superior to the single-shot carbines we carried. Finally, and probably the most important of all, we were badly outgeneraled. Like it or not, the Sioux fought a much smarter battle. As a consequence, we took a savage whipping. All of which is history now, a sad and needless part of the past. So, what about Pop?"

Jonathan Peabody leaned back, pushed a hand across his chin, and spoke with slow care. "It was pretty late at night. You know how it was with Pop—how he kept the store open long after most of the town had closed up for the night. Not for his own profit, understand—but for the possible needs of others. Like a rancher from the far-back range, reaching town real late yet hoping to pick up a sack or two of supplies. Or maybe a drifting granger layout in need of food for a passel of hungry kids, which was something old Pop refused to even think about—a hungry kid having to go to bed that way. Which was Pop Worley for you—always thinking of the other fellow instead of himself."

Hilliard nodded, his eyes deeply charged with the shadows of regret. "How well I remember all those things—how well! Like the day I first saw Pop. I was a six-year-old kid, orphaned when our wagon overturned in a flooding stream. I lived because another wagon man managed to snake me out. He was a good man and kind enough to me, but a lone, wandering teamster was no way fixed to care decently for a single kid. So one day, when he happened to stop at Pop's store, he asked Pop if he knew where he might find a good home for me.

"Pop said sure he could, and he did. He took me in for his own. No real father could have done more for me. Somehow he found time to do so many worthwhile things for me, such as teaching me some book learning and how to be a good citizen. All I am or ever will be, I owe to Pop Worley. In his early years he had seen service in the cavalry, so when I was old enough, he suggested a hitch in the Seventh for me, saying that four years of military training was good for anyone, and that when the hitch was over with, I'd be ready to face the world. Well, it is—and I am. And the first chore I take on as a civilian is to track down the miserable whelp who robbed and killed one of the best men who ever drew breath. That's a promise! Now get on about the holdup and the shooting."

Again Jonathan Peabody spoke with the slow care of one laying out every item of an incident in its exact sequence. "Like I said, it was late. Four of us had a low-limit game of stud poker going in the hotel bar. Tom Roberts, Pete Logan, Doc Wherry, and myself. It had started as five-handed, with Hutch Baker sitting in. But Hutch had a mare in his corral that was about to foal, and he wanted to keep an eye on her, so he left a little early. He'd hardly hit the street when a single shot sounded down at the store. Right after, somebody ran out of the place, hit a saddle, and lit out, hell-for-leather.

"Hutch cut for the store where he found Pop down behind the counter, his old .44 store gun on the floor beside him. Hutch hotfooted it back for the rest of us. Pop was still alive when we got there, but though Doc Wherry did all he could, it was no use. The cash drawer was open right above where Pop lay. He'd been checking the day's take when this fellow charged in waving a gun. Much too salty to stand still for robbery, Pop grabbed his store gun off the counter shelf. But the old man didn't have a chance—he was shot down before he could pull the trigger.

"Still conscious, Pop told how it had happened and gave what description he could of the killer, which wasn't much except for one solid point. The killer was average tall with a blue bandanna across his face. He kept his gun ready in his right hand while scooping what he could from the cash drawer with his left. Looking up from where he lay, Pop had a clear view of that left hand. And there were only four fingers on it. The middle finger was missing. To his last and final breath Pop kept telling us again and again about that left hand with the missing finger."

Eyes charged with a hard, cold light, Jud Hilliard stared straight ahead, a man peering into the future while laying out words that were full of a bleak and bitter purpose.

"Not much to go on, but I'll be looking for that left hand, and no matter how long it takes or how far I have to travel, I'll find it." Shifting restlessly, he added harshly, "What did you people do then?"

Jonathan Peabody shrugged helpless shoulders. "What could we do? The killer was long gone into the night. As town marshal, Pete Logan's official authority reaches only to the town limits. Just the same, Pete strapped on his gun, took one of Hutch Baker's best horses, and spent the rest of the night and all the next day scouting every trail between here and Haden Creek Junction. Came up with nothing, of course. Been a sheer miracle otherwise, for this is a mighty big and empty country, as you well know. One that can easily swallow a lone rider. That's the all of it, Jud."

"Maybe for you—but not for me!" Hilliard burst out savagely.

A quick flush stained the banker's cheeks. Glimpsing this and understanding why, Hilliard added quick words in a milder tone. "Sorry, Mr. Peabody. I said that wrong and didn't mean it the way it sounded. I'm sure you people did all you reasonably could. But what happened to old Pop has me all chewed up inside."

Jonathan Peabody nodded quietly. "I understand. It has a lot of us chewed up inside. But life goes on, and we have no other out but to go along with it. We all have things to do and take care of. Like the future of the store. It's all yours now, you know. Long ago Pop drew up a will right on my desk, leaving everything to you. And folks hereabouts are more than anxious for the store to be open for business again. A solid future waiting for you there, Jud."

Hilliard shook his head quickly and definitely. "Not for me. Was Pop alive and still running it, I might stand the store for a little time but not for long. What I saw and went through during my service hitch knocked all idea of store work out of me. Changed my thinking on a lot of things. Put a restlessness in me too. Telling me to get out and take a look at the rest of the world. There must be somebody else around who could take over the store and make a real go of it."

Peabody nodded. "There is. Ed Dorris, who on occasion helped Pop while you were away. Ed's honest, a good, solid family man. He knows the business and likes it."

"Perfect. Go get him," Hilliard urged quickly. "On any kind of deal that makes for a fair shake all around."

"Sure you want it so?"

"Plenty sure. Without Pop in it I couldn't stand the store."

"Something else," Peabody reminded. "There's considerable money due you. Most of it on deposit with me. What about that?"

"Leave it there. I'll take enough along to last me for a while. Comes I need more, I'll write you from wherever I happen to be."

Draining a final cup of coffee, Jonathan Peabody closely studied Jud Hilliard over the rim of it. He nodded, as though convinced of something. "Boy," he said, "you're really going after that fellow— the killer—aren't you?"

Hilliard pushed back his chair, got out his pipe, and began packing it. "That's it," he said steadily, "that's the all of it. However long it takes, however far I have to go. It means, of course, that it's a cold, cold trail I'll have to work out, so it could take time. But I've got lots of time. Lots of time!"

C H A P T E R
2

*E*ARLY the next morning Jud Hilliard was on his way, a lean, deeply tanned, hard-jawed man on a big red horse. He realized he was searching for a man he had never seen and whose name he did not know. And he had only a general description that would have fit many thousands of men. Except for one clue: the man Jud Hilliard wanted was minus the middle finger of his left hand. It was the brand that a thief and murderer could not hide—the brand he would carry to his grave.

Hilliard had no illusions as to the challenges that lay ahead. This was something that would take time—lots of time—together with patience and dogged persistence. Where to start, where to dredge up the first lead? For a time after he left Meridian it seemed that he was never to find that first lead. But finally he came upon it. He was over a tawdry little bar in a lonely way-station.

To Hilliard's careful question about the man with the missing finger, the bartender answered, "I saw such a hand. The owner of it was rolling the dice with me for a drink. He shot the dice with his right hand, scooped them up with his left. That's how I happened to notice the missing finger. He was a surly sort, a short sport, because when I beat him, he didn't like it a bit. You after him for something?"

Hilliard nodded. "That's right. For murder and robbery. Which way did he ride from here?"

"He came in from the east. He didn't head back that way."

"So he was traveling west," Hilliard said. "Now, I won't shake you for a drink, but I'd like to buy you one."

When the drinks were poured, the bartender lifted his glass. "Here's hopin' you catch up with him!"

Tenacious as a wolf nosing the sign of blood, Hilliard went on from there, crossing plains and mountains, asking his guarded, but ever seeking questions at the saloon bars and eating-house counters of a succession of isolated backcountry cow towns and in the bunkhouses of lonely ranches. West ran the trail, ever west, through rugged prairie and deep into high desert. It was a trail that at times grew so faint that Hilliard feared he'd lost it entirely. Yet always, as though some capricious fate had decided to take part in matters, some last-minute hint would crop up to lead him on, ever on, with purpose and fervor renewed.

The previous night, with the nearest supply point many miles behind and his meager food pack starkly empty, he had spread his blanket in a seemingly endless sea of sage, and, hungry and thirsty, slept fitfully under this sage desert's vast and lonely reach of stars. Now, on this, the morning of still another day, as he pressed doggedly ahead a thin drift of wood smoke came to meet him. Following this lure eagerly took him across a low roll of country and down into a little basin where the everlasting sage finally gave way to some half dozen acres of green, grassy meadowland, lying around a water seep.

Here burned the source of the smoke. Beside the fire stood a battered chuck wagon. At its lowered tailgate, a gunnysack apron sagging around a gaunt middle, flour dusting the bared forearms, labored an ancient, grizzled old black man. Off to one side a team of horses grazed.

Turning to watch Hilliard ride in, the old Negro showed a sharp, intent scrutiny before speaking.

"Howdy, stranger! Somethin' I can do for you?"

Hilliard tipped his head toward the spring. "A little water for both my horse and myself. We're pretty thirsty."

The black man waved an arm. "O' course. Water's free. He'p yo'self."

The water was a bit alkaline, but not enough to matter greatly. Rider and mount both drank deeply, after which the red horse began reaching eagerly for grass, a move the black man did not miss.

"That there is one hungry bronc," he remarked. "Kinda ga'nted too. Take the saddle off him and let him roll and graze. Plenty of grass, and it's free, same as the water."

Following this suggestion, Jud Hilliard moved over to the fire where he underwent another careful appraisal.

"You runnin' from somethin' or somebody?"

Hilliard smiled faintly. "May look that way, but I'm not."

As he spoke, his glance dropped to the fire where a couple of pots and a dutch oven were tucked against the flames. The black man read the thought behind the glance and made another blunt demand.

"When did you vittle last?"

Again Hilliard's faint smile showed. "Considerable time ago. Which has me wondering what's in those pots?"

"Hi—hi!" The old black fellow cackled a merry laugh. "Ol' Zeke—that's me. Zeke Borders. Had you figgered jes' same as your bronc. Both kinda ga'nted, like you hadn't been feedin' too regular lately."

While speaking, he deftly shuffled plate and cup and eating utensils from the wagon's chuck box. "Dig in," he invited. "They're beans and coffee in the pots an' short ribs in the oven."

There was also a pan of brown-crusted dough-god biscuits, freshly cooked. Seated cross-legged by the fire, Jud Hilliard ate and drank eagerly. The first edge of raw hunger satisfied, he looked up at his benefactor.

"Zeke Borders, you're the finest gentleman I know. What can I say, besides 'thanks'?"

Again the old fellow gave out his thin, high-pitched laugh.

"Ain't no need of thankin'. That's some of Boss Tim Rowland's beef you chewin' on, and he won't mind. I been workin' for Boss Tim better'n thirty years now. 'Spect I'll likely die, workin' for Boss Tim."

Hilliard's glance took in the layout. "Where's your outfit?"

"Should be showin' about noon," Zeke Borders said. "I allus throw camp down here when the boys is fixin' to work out the roughs over south."

The sun, steadily climbing, pushed its flat rays against a dark lift of country well out to the west. "What's that country, Zeke?"

The old black man sobered. "Them's the Bannock Hills. Ain't never been in them and ain't fixin' to go there, either. Nothin' in them for Old Zeke Borders. That there's trouble country. I hear'n tell that in them there hills, folks are feudin' again. Folks like Caleb Marion and Sam Wade are still fussin' at each other over the war. Which don't make a lick of sense to me, and it's no place for a feller like me to go mixin' in. I ain't aimin' to get stamped down flat—no, sir! You figgerin' on goin' there?"

Hilliard's eyes narrowed thoughtfully. "Depends. If I can save time and distance by going through those hills, then I will."

Again Old Zeke fixed Hilliard with that direct and steady appraisal. "While back, I ask's you was you runnin' from somebody. You said no, you wasn't. Now I'm askin'—is you chasin' somebody?"

This ancient, kindly, old black man, with his blunt and disturbing honesty, deserved an equally honest answer, and Hilliard gave him one.

"Amounts to that, Zeke."

"How come? You a lawman?"

"No," Hilliard admitted quietly. "But I am on the trail of a fellow who robbed and, in cold blood, shot down one of the finest men that ever walked the earth, a man who once took in a small orphan boy and raised him as he might one of his own, giving that boy a fair chance at life. I was that boy, Zeke, and I'm looking for the damned renegade who killed my foster father. A renegade who's missing the middle finger on his left hand. Does that fit anybody you know of who might have come through here?"

Hilliard needed no spoken admission to know the truth, as Old Zeke had visibly started, then went very still for a little time. He straightened his shoulders before speaking with sober restraint.

"Sayin' all that is so, what you is on now is vengeance business. An' friend, that ain't never good business."

"Then would you say that you believe out-and-out robbery and murder should go unpunished?" pressed Hilliard quickly.

Old Zeke considered this, pursing his lips, his brow furrowed with thought. He scrubbed a hand across his face and let his shoulders drop in a fatalistic shrug. "Puttin' things thataway, then I reckon you is right in goin' after that no-good feller."

"And you have seen the one I'm looking for? Last trace I had of him, he was headed this way."

Zeke Borders nodded his gaunt and grizzled head. "Feller with a hand like that was through here some time back. I fed him, same as I'm feedin' you. But there was a look about him I didn't much like—for it was sorta shifty and mean. Must say I felt better after he pulled out. And he sure had only four fingers on his left hand—middle one was missin'. I did some wonderin' about that."

"It's the one sure angle that's enabled me to trail him this far, Zeke," Hilliard said. "Which way did he head from here?"

"He cut for them Bannock Hills. I told him it was trouble country, but he paid me no mind. Now I 'spect you will sure nuff head for them hills too?"

"Right away," Hilliard said. Finished with his food, he stood up, arms spread wide. "Zeke, I'm beginning to live again. I won't insult you by offering to pay for that meal. But I sure am grateful to you and Boss Tim. Next time you see him, you tell him that!" Again he indicated the lift of hill country to the west. "About how far would you say, Zeke?"

Zeke speculated, frowning. "Man ridin' steady might hit there jes' about sundown. That bronc of yours a good traveler?"

"None better," Hilliard declared. "The big fellow and me—we've been together a long time and have seen a lot of country."

He saddled the big red horse and swung into the leather. Now he paused to look down at the ancient Negro. "I'm saying it again, Zeke Borders. You're the finest man I know."

Again came Old Zeke's high-pitched, infectious

laugh. "Ha ha! 'Spect the way you is feelin' right now is the difference between havin' a full belly instead of an empty one."

While speaking, Zeke had been putting odds and ends into a clean flour sack. He lifted the sack up to Hilliard.

"Jes' a little somethin' to keep you from sleepin' hungry tonight should them Bannock Hills shape up too plumb high and empty. You is a likely young feller, so wherever you go and whatever you figger you have to do, jes' remember this. Ol' Zeke Borders is hopin' you come through safe!"

As Jud Hilliard and the big red horse pushed on and on, the never-ending sage ran away and away, seemingly without limit. But both the hours and the miles fell behind them, horse and rider chased by an ever-lengthening shadow.

Squinting into the glare of a declining sun, Jud Hilliard saw the country ahead hump higher and higher, deciding that the judgment of time and distance by Zeke Borders was working out to near exactness. For with day's end less than an hour away, the beginnings of hill country now lay before him.

It had been a tiring trip, lasting out the miles, but here the sage was thinning, giving way to a scatter of junipers, while just beyond, reposing in the blue and lavender mist of sundown, marched green and shadowy ranks of timber.

A dip in the even run of the trees suggested a fold in the flank of the hills, and seeking this, Hilliard reined into the mouth of a gulch, meeting with the cool, moist breath of mountain water. It was only a shallow little pool, but the big red horse reached for it eagerly, drinking long and deeply before lifting a dripping muzzle to chuffer in weary contentment.

Hilliard shook the reins. "Get along a little further, Red. We'll find more water higher up."

There was a steep, narrow game trail to climb, but it led into a small flat where there was more water, a fair amount of graze, and space enough for a man to throw down camp for the night. Moving quickly against the onward rush of twilight, Hilliard unsaddled, turned the horse loose to roll and graze, then gathered an armload of dry windfall from the timber round about. Soon a crackling, cheery camp fire was pushing back the creeping shadows.

From his meager pack Hilliard brought out a small, use-blackened pot, scooped water into it, added a handful of the coffee so thoughtfully provided by Zeke Borders, and tucked the pot against the flames. When the brew steamed and turned over, he made his supper of it, together with some cold steak and biscuits from the same flour sack Old Zeke had provided.

His hunger satisfied, he crouched beside the fire, pipe between his teeth, and watched the flames gutter down into a bed of coals that glittered like dusted rubies in the ashes. Later, rolled in his blanket and with his saddle for a pillow, he watched the starlight filter through the timber tops and listened to the great silences of space close down about him.

For a time, as weary as he was, Jud Hilliard lay wide-eyed, sleep pushed aside by the crush of reaching thoughts. So much had come his way in the past fourteen hours. That morning, far back in the wilderness of sage, determination for further pursuit of his quarry had faltered almost to the point of defeat. Only the ghost of a stubborn purpose had sent him on to meet up with Zeke Borders. There, besides the food and drink supplied by kindly Old Zeke, he'd picked up the best and surest lead he'd known since his search began: a lead that a four-fingered man had come through this way. Though that time was now months gone, the fact remained that he had been through here, heading into these Bannock Hills. Maybe the fellow had gone right through. But again, because these hills were trouble country, even violent country, as Zeke Borders had emphasized, it could be just the kind of haven such a fugitive would remain in.

One point Hilliard had considered many times was whether the fugitive had in some way picked up a hint of the vengeance-bound pursuer that was on his trail. If so, when or where would he ever stop running and make a stand and risk a showdown through gunsmoke with the stubborn pursuer? Only the future could answer these questions. On this conclusion Jud Hilliard sought and found sleep, still wondering but also still grimly committed to the chase.

He awakened to a dim, chill world full of early-morning mist that sifted ghostlike through the timber. Working swiftly against the chill, he broke camp, saddled up, and sent the big red horse climbing toward the crest of the country ahead, a goal he could only guess at, being hemmed in here by marching ranks of timber. In time he began catching glimpses of a morning sky now showing a ruddy flush of the color of sunrise, after which the world brightened steadily.

The timber began giving way to an occasional mountain meadow, and beyond a shallow timber basin lay one such meadow, this one with movement in it, movement that caused Hilliard to rein up sharply, rearing high in his saddle as he watched.

The movement was a horse, a light-colored animal, a buckskin, and the manner with which it moved, head jerking up and down, suggested one of two possible causes. Either reins were dragging and being stepped on or the animal had a badly lamed front leg. It was still too soon to be certain of cause, but not too soon to mark the fact that the saddle the horse carried was an empty one.

Reared high in his saddle, Hilliard made a spare, yet solid figure, a man who filled his clothes completely and whose sharpened glance was alert and probing. The past several months of steady saddle travel had made him lean, while turning his deeply weathered features slightly hawkish. His denim jumper was faded and threadbare, and now, being tightly pulled across shoulders and chest by the twist of his poised body, showed the swell of hard muscle under it. Here, as he watched, nothing in his immediate scope moved save that lurching, stumbling horse yonder, while all around the silence piled up until it became the hushed, yet vaguely whispering stillness peculiar to timbered hills.

In him both experience and instinct were at work, the one suggesting that a horse wandering around under empty saddle could well mean trouble; the other hinting strongly that something of the sort now lay right before him. Held by his thoughts, Hilliard stood statue-still, his glance again raking the visible world, all his senses keen and searching.

Trouble country, these hills—so Zeke Borders had branded them. Trouble country. Hilliard considered his possible courses of action.

When a decision came to him, it was abrupt and sure. He sent the big red horse down and across the timber basin and into the meadow clearing. Here the other horse—a buckskin, sure enough—lifted a sagging head, whinnying plaintively as it made its painful, three-legged approach. It took but a single glance for Hilliard to read the clear cause of its stumbling, uneven gait.

Between knee and shoulder the buckskin's near front leg was all one great raw and livid wound: leg bone shattered; the lower part of the leg swinging loose. Here was no accidental trailway injury. One thing, and one thing only, could be responsible for such a savage wreckage of flesh and bone and sinew. Here, unmistakably, was the work of bullets!

The buckskin tried a further, unsteady approach, again whinnying in a way that swiftly darkened Jud Hilliard's glance with pity. For here was something beyond any hope of repair. Nothing could be done for the unfortunate possessor of that shattered leg, save the final, demanding act of mercy.

How far, Hilliard wondered, would the sound of a shot carry? How deeply might it commit a man? He shrugged the question aside. No matter! You did not ride away, leaving a thing of this sort undone. It was an obligation of moral decency he had to face up to. When or where, now or later, made no difference. It was something that had to be done.

He drew the gun at his hip, thumbed back the hammer, and lifted the weapon into line, holding it so for a careful moment to make quite certain of the result. When the big Colt gun reared in recoil, the report a heavy thud of sound against the surrounding timber, the buckskin collapsed instantly, all terror, all pain and suffering ended.

Snorting, Hilliard's big red would have swung away, but Hilliard hauled it back, slowly holstering his gun while looking down at the buckskin. Hilliard saw more than he had at first. Along the buckskin's mane and down the side of its neck were further smears of turgid, half-dried blood, with no visible wound to account for it. Going far over in his saddle to make certain of this, Hilliard then straightened and put the big red horse to circling, while his glance searched the earth, seeking the trail the buckskin had followed.

What with dragging hoofprints and the blood from the shattered leg that the trail made plain, surely the horse had come into the meadow clearing on the upper side. From here the somber sign led steadily uphill, past a small aspen swamp to a ridge top where a narrow road ran its twisting way through warm-boled ponderosa pine. And here, only a few yards from where the buckskin had left the road, Jud Hilliard found what he was afraid he would.

The rider sprawled on his back was young, with a draining pallor underlying the slight hint of swarthiness in his features. Black hair, rumpled and shaggy, spread low over his forehead. One jean-clad leg was outstretched and straight, the other hiked up a trifle, knee bent. The holster belted around his lean middle was empty, the gun that had once filled it lying just beyond an outflung hand. The front of a faded blue calico shirt showed a soggy patch of crimson.

Hilliard's first impression was that here lay a rider who surely was dead. Yet even as this thought registered there sounded the faintest of moans from scarcely moving lips, while that bent leg slowly straightened. Hesitating only long enough to lay an intent, searching glance all around him and finding nothing there but the quietude of the timbered hills, Hilliard was swiftly out of his saddle, kneeling and peeling back that soggy shirt: The bullet hole was there, dark and blue and ominous in a pucker of welted flesh. The slug had gone all the way through, and blood was pooled under the exit wound.

It was not the first time Jud Hilliard had seen life slipping away from a man, so he knew that if this young fellow was to have any chance at all, that deadly drain had to be staunched. Nearby lay an old, downed log, heavily furred with damp moss. Stripping off big handfuls of this, Hilliard wadded it thickly over both entrance and exit wounds, binding it in place with strips torn from a bloody shirt.

With every touch he expected to have death under his hands. Yet when he finished, life was still there. But he knew it would not stay there should he try to get the wounded rider across a saddle. If this youngster was to be moved at all, it would have to be by some other means. Shucking out of his own jumper, Jud Hilliard spread it across the bandaged chest, murmuring his concern.

"Doing the best I can for you, friend!"

He caught up the rider's gun, flipped open the loading gate, and spun the cylinder. It was a .41 Bisley Model Colt, and one load had been fired from it. He shoved the weapon into one of his saddlebags, then stepped astride with the big red horse jigging restlessly in the dust of the road. Now came the big question. Which way?

Up above, the road climbed narrowly through thickening timber. Below, it dropped in a series of sweeping curves into what appeared to be the beginnings of more open country. Hilliard put the big red into the down grade and presently found the timber giving way on either side. Abruptly after this the road broke into the clear, and a man could see far.

Here was open grass country, the hills sweeping back to cradle a shallow, long-reaching valley, and out there ahead, at the base of the western slope, buildings and the sprawl of corrals marked a ranch headquarters. Cutting past this, the road drove straight down the heart of the valley. Along that road, just ahead of a trailing banner of tawny dust, a spring wagon rolled behind a jogging team. Jud Hilliard met up with the rig just as it was about to take the turnoff to the ranch.

An elderly woman rode the wagon seat. Responding to Hilliard's raised arm, she hauled up her team and set the brake. She was buttoned to the chin in an old linen duster, and a floppy-brimmed Stetson covered her gray head. Her eyes were sharp and direct as she looked him over before making a curt inquiry in a tone as cool and direct as her glance.

"Something you wanted?"

"Maybe a loan of your team and wagon, ma'am" —Hilliard touched the brim of his hat as he spoke—"because there's a young fellow lying in the road back yonder in the timber with a bullet hole through him."

Quick concern brought the woman up straight on the wagon seat. "You mean, he's dead?"

"Wasn't when I left him, but skating close. Did what I could for him, but to try to carry him across a saddle would surely finish him. Hauled in a wagon he might have a chance."

Again her shrewd glance questioned Hilliard. "Young, you say? What does he look like?"

"Lean, lanky kid. Black hair. Me, I'm Jud Hilliard and new to this country, so wouldn't have any idea who he is or why he's been shot.

All I know is that he's losing more blood than he can afford. So if we're to get anywhere with him, it will have to be fast."

The woman kicked off her brake. "Lead out—I'll follow!"

Hilliard set the red horse to it. Behind him, under the urging of voice and whip, the wagon team came at a gallop, and when they topped out above the curves, they were sweating and blowing. Stepping quickly out of her wagon, the gray-haired woman joined Hilliard beside the prone rider. Her taut exclamation was charged with a meaning that Hilliard did not miss. His head swung.

"You know him?"

"Yes. It is Caleb Marion's youngest son, Parker. Being new to this valley, you wouldn't know what this may lead to. But if the boy dies, the result could be terrible. Thank heaven he still lives. We'll get him into the wagon. I'll make room for him."

She had been hauling a sack of flour and other assorted food items. These things she pushed well up front, then took a folded blanket from the wagon seat and spread it across the rear of the wagon bed. With anxious care she helped Hilliard lift the wounded man onto the blanket.

"He's still with us, ma'am," Hilliard said encouragingly. "But sure in need of a doctor's care. How far to one?"

"Much too far" was the sober reply. "At Keystone, way out past the northern end of these mountains. Could be days before such a doctor could be located and brought in. But there is a woman in our valley who is very able in matters of this sort. Her name is Hester Loring, and she runs a little eating house in town. Go locate her and send her out to my ranch. Tell her that Molly Clement is waiting for her—and why. Also, don't believe any snide remarks some might make about her, as she is a far better and kinder person than those who would make such remarks."

Hilliard went into his saddle. "And this valley town?"

"Willow Creek. And I've a ranch hand to help me with this boy until Hester arrives."

Hilliard swung the red horse around. "All right, big feller, you've been wanting to run, so get at it!"

CHAPTER 3

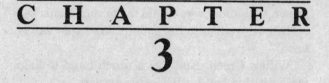

THE big red ran with an effortless stride that cut distance down swiftly, and the farther Jud Hilliard rode, the more the valley opened out. On either side the ridges reared, dark with timber, and slashed here and there with shadowed defiles. In several places well marked trails broke away from the road, leading into these dark, timbered reaches, telling of more big, wild country farther back. Short of town a pair of small, willow-lined creeks broke from the timber to converge into a single larger stream that slid past the edge of town.

The town of Willow Creek was an irregular

scatter of buildings clustered around one main street and two shorter cross streets. Reining the big red down to a jog, Hilliard passed the familiar reek of corrals and a livery barn before pulling in at the hitch rail of a building identified by a swinging, weather-faded sign:

WILLOW CREEK SUPPLY
Homer Gort, Prop.

The hitch rail held two saddle mounts, one of them a strongly marked little black-and-white calico pony. As Hilliard put the big red in beside the calico mount a ripple of bright, feminine laughter sounded, and a young woman stepped from the store, drawing on a pair of riding gloves while making an amused remark over her shoulder to someone behind her.

She was slender in a blouse and divided skirt. She carried her head high, her slim shoulders pridefully erect as she moved to the outer edge of the store's platform porch with an easy, natural grace. Her bared head was sleekly dark in marked contrast to the yellow-gold scarf looped casually around her neck. Hilliard was struck by her beauty.

The man who followed her from the store, though booted and spurred, was dressed considerably better than any average saddle hand. Both shirt and trousers were of a fine weave of tan serge, and his hat was an expensive roll-brimmed white Stetson. He was a roan-headed man who carried his shoulders with a challenging swing. His answer to his companion was an amused rumble that shaped a husky background to the girl's lighter laughter.

At the sight of Jud Hilliard both these people turned quiet, measuring him with a fixed scrutiny that held some wonder, and on the man's part, what struck Hilliard as a shadow of some instinctive suspicion. In deference to the girl, Hilliard lifted a finger to his hat brim as he spoke.

"I'm looking for a lady by the name of Hester Loring. Could you folks tell me where I might find her?"

Their reaction was startling. Mildly curious before, the girl's glance went quickly distant while the man's reply was curt and colored by a covert sneer.

"There is such a person in town. But I wouldn't know about the lady angle. Old and close friend of yours, maybe?"

Mindful of what the woman with the spring wagon had told him, Hilliard's cheeks tightened.

"The lady—and I said *lady*—is needed at the Clement ranch where she may save a man's life. There's a young fellow out there with a bullet through him—a rider named Parker Marion.

Now, are you going to tell me where I can find Hester Loring or do we waste time making cheap, damn-fool smart talk while that young fellow dies?"

It was the girl who answered him. She came flashing off the store platform, her face white with shocked concern as she looked up at him.

"Did you say Parker Marion? You're sure of that?"

"It's how Molly Clement named him," Hilliard nodded.

With an increasingly stricken look the girl freed the calico pony's tie and flung herself into the saddle. Even as she swung the calico pony around she was calling to the man who was behind her.

"Nile—get word to Garr or Wilce. Find them and tell them. And hurry. Hurry!"

Her last words faded as she tore away, her pony stretched out and running like a scared wolf. To Hilliard's questioning glance Nile gave a husky—and now, civil—explanation.

"Miss Cody Marion. Parker is her younger brother."

"Too bad," Hilliard said. "But it was Hester Loring that Molly Clement asked for. Where will I find her? And she'll need some means of travel to get where she is needed. Also, time counts plenty in this matter."

Nile nodded. He had a face so broad, it gave a

thrusting tilt to his chin. Above the thick swell
of his neck his ears were small and tucked cat-
close to his head, while his cheeks showed the
high flush of lusty living. Now he said, "I'll
round up a rig for her. The place you'll likely
find her is the Elite, an eating house next to the
hotel, straight on down the street."

Jud Hilliard sent the red horse along to a
small place of business that fronted on the street.
Out in back were living quarters, neatly fenced
and surrounded by a well-kept, flower-brightened
yard. The woman who answered the door at
Hilliard's knock carried a hint of guarded wari-
ness in her glance, but when she spoke, her
words fell softly and quietly.

"If it is food you want, it is much too early for
supper. Do you mind waiting"

She was one who had left her girlhood years
behind her while still retaining the instinctive
grace and much of the bloom of those earlier
years. Her skin was fair and touched with soft
color, and a crown of brown hair framed features
that were warm and regular. Her eyes were clear
hazel and reflected the serene steadiness of one
who had met a full share of life's rougher moments and who now faced the future with the
confidence of a sure and settled wisdom.

"It's not food, ma'am," Hilliard explained. "A
ranch woman named Molly Clement sent me
looking for Hester Loring. Because there is a

wounded man—gunshot—now at the Clement ranch. Young rider named Marion, Parker Marion. Molly Clement said that Hester Loring would know what to do in a case of this sort. You are the person I'm looking for?"

"Yes. I am Hester Loring." The answer was even, quiet. "But it is fairer to say that I know how to *try* to do something for a wounded person— but nothing more. Of only one thing am I completely sure, and this word you bring confirms it: that so many men are fools before they are anything else. So blindly intent on destroying each other for no good reason." She paused to nod slightly, as though emphasizing some dark wisdom arrived at through experience. "In my time I have helped mend several of them, and I'm not too sure they were worth the effort. So now it is Parker Marion, you say? Which says that the old madness has again begun to scourge these hills. I'll need some means of getting out to Molly's ranch."

"Fellow down at the store is having a rig sent for you," Jud Hilliard said.

"That would be Homer Gort?"

Hilliard shook his head. "Fellow I'm speaking of is named Nile Somebody. I heard him called so. Big fellow, heavy-jawed and dressed a little too fancy for a regular saddle hand."

Hester Loring's lip curled. "Mr. Nile Starkey, eh? He might send a rig, but he'd never bring it.

And probably do neither if it wasn't a Marion who is hurt. But no matter—we'll do our best. The boy, Parker—he's badly wounded?"

"Very bad," Hilliard said soberly. "You could be making the drive out there for nothing."

She searched him with a keen, gauging glance. "Of course, you are not the one who shot him?"

"No," Hilliard said. "I just happened to be the one who found him."

She shook a sorrowful head. "Not a bad lad, Parker. A mite wild, perhaps, but that is just the youth of it. Also, of course, just slightly touched with that dark Marion pride. Now, if this were his cousin, Hube, who at best is a miserable whelp, I'd be inclined to beg off and do nothing. But Parker—he's Caleb Marion's youngest and pretty much the favorite of the whole family." Again she shook a sorrowful head. "My, oh, my—I do so hate to see this thing start up again. Why can't men learn to live at peace with one another? Well, I'll go collect my things."

She turned back toward the rear of the house. Hilliard went over and leaned against the sweaty shoulder of the big red horse while getting out his pipe and loading it. He had it lit and drawing well when a buckboard and team came speeding along the street, driven by a wizened little man with bird-bright eyes. The little man hauled up and hopped out of the rig, moving with a pronounced limp. In a voice as pinched and reedy as his own small body, he had a quick question for Jud Hilliard.

"You the feller who brought the word about Park Marion?"

Hilliard nodded. "That's right."

"He'd been shot? Somebody gunned him?"

"Seems to be the size of it."

"Bad!" exclaimed the little man. "Mighty damn bad! Should this set old Caleb Marion off again, which is more'n likely, then there sure will be supreme hell to pay!"

When Hester Loring reappeared, she had a large, fully packed basket on one arm. At her side stood a big-eyed little lad of four or five. She passed her free arm around the youngster with a warm protectiveness; bent and brushed her lips against the little fellow's cheek while murmuring soft words of endearment.

"I won't be gone too long, Terry. Be a good boy until Mother gets back." She straightened, her next words for the old man.

"You and Terry will have to manage things for a time, Abner. If matters out at the Clement ranch are as bad as seems likely, I could be staying the night and a large part of tomorrow. Don't be too concerned over having to rustle a meal or two for the hungry ones. You've done it before, so you'll do all right."

The old fellow bobbed a grizzled head. "Sure we will, Miss Hester. Don't you worry. Just stay close to that hurt boy out there as long as necessary. And good luck!"

Hester Loring hoisted her basket to one end of the buckboard seat, then climbed in and picked up the reins, looking down at the little man who had brought the rig. "Thanks, Skeeter. I don't know who is to pay for the use of this, but you've my permission to charge it to Nile Starkey. At which he'd probably bleed a little, when and if he ever pays."

"Ain't askin' pay from nobody, Miss Hester," the little man declared. "This trip is on the house."

Hester Loring smiled at him, murmuring, "Ever the generous one—that's you, Skeeter." Her expression sobered as she turned her glance to Jud Hilliard. "I doubt anyone will thank you for your part in the affair, though of course they certainly should. Far more likely you'll have reason to wish you'd never seen or heard of Parker Marion or any of the rest of the family, for that matter."

She kicked off the brake, clucked to the team, swung the buckboard through a wheel-skidding turn, and rolled out of town.

Hilliard looked after her for a moment, then put some questions to the little man beside him.

"You work at the livery and wagon yard?"

"Sure do—I own it" was the peppery reply. "Me, I'm Skeeter Dahl. Who are you?"

Hilliard had to grin at this feisty directness. "Hilliard, here. Jud Hilliard. You got room in your layout for this horse of mine?"

"Sure have...plenty!" Skeeter Dahl said. "Always room for another good one."

They went back along the street to the stable, Hilliard leading the big red. Limping and hopping along, Skeeter Dahl kept pace, all the while explaining the reason for his infirmity.

"Used to drive stage out of Keystone. Got a late start one day, and by the time I hit the Logan Canyon grade, it was near dark. Met up with a raunchy old black bear with a couple of cubs. The ornery old devil figgered she owned the road and was plenty ready to argue the point. She began whoofin' and snarlin' and poppin' her teeth so mean and ugly, the team spooked and took me and the stage off the road, piling things up real bad in the canyon creek. I laid there all that night and part of the next day before a freight outfit happened along to find me and haul me back to Keystone.

"The doc at Keystone did his best, but he couldn't make me into a whole man again, so my stage drivin' days were over. I'd saved a little money, enough to start up a livery business here in Willow Creek. Won't ever get rich. Won't starve, either. Get by pretty good in spite of this bum leg." Skeeter Dahl broke off long enough to let out a thin, dry chuckle. "We're two of a kind, Caleb Marion and me—both of us gimpy-legged. But I'm better off than Caleb, for, such as it is, I still got a whole leg. But Caleb, all he's got is a wooden stub. Came off second-best with a cannonball in Pickett's charge up Little Roundtop at Gettysburg. And still a diehard Johnny Reb, Caleb is."

Abruptly the little man's attention switched to a new observation. He looked up at Hilliard's horse. "Friend, this horse of yours is sure a big one. What does he stand, a good sixteen hands?"

"And then some," Hilliard said. "And he's earned a clean, well-bedded stall, a good currying and brushing down, plus a big feed of oats and a mangerful of hay."

"Cost you half a dollar," Skeeter Dahl chirruped.

Jud Hilliard handed over the money, unstrapped his saddlebags, and yoked them across his shoulder. "Where can a man rent a decent room and bed for the night?"

Skeeter pointed. "Valley Hotel. Cluny Grimes sets a pretty fair table, too, when he sets his mind to it. But me, I generally do my eating at Hester Loring's place."

From a scant two-storied height the Valley Hotel looked down on the rest of the town. Heading for it, Jud Hilliard saw Nile Starkey leave the place and angle across the street toward a sign that indicated the Gilt Edge Bar. In passing, Starkey showed him another slanting glance that seemed to carry more than average curiosity. And from the doorway of the Willow Creek Supply store a stocky, round-bodied man in a flour-dusted apron watched Hilliard all the way to the hotel. Keenly aware of the two, Hilliard puzzled over them for a moment before shrugging them aside. He was a stranger in a plainly hostile land, a land he had arrived in under strained and violent conditions. Therefore, he realized, such questioning attitudes were to be expected.

The man who faced Jud Hilliard across the meager extent of the hotel's register desk had a pointed jaw; large, wide-spread ears; and a pair of anxious, protuberant eyes under pale brows. The overall effect made Hilliard think of a startled, half-frightened rabbit.

"Room for the night and maybe a meal or two," Hilliard said, pulling the register around and signing with a bold, slanting hand: Judson Hilliard. Burnt Corral, Idaho.

"Cluny Grimes, here," said the rabbit-faced man, studying Hilliard's signature. Murmuring, he added, "Burnt Corral, eh? Thought I knew the Idaho country pretty well. Never heard of that place, though."

Hilliard grinned. "Lots of people haven't. Just a wide place in the trail, and so close to the state line, nobody knows for sure if it is in Idaho or Oregon. But everybody has to be from someplace, and Burnt Corral is good enough for me, being the last place I slept in a bed. Now, about that room?"

"Number three, upstairs," Cluny Grimes directed. "Beds are clean, food first-class, and prices fair. Room for the night is a dollar; by the week, five dollars. In advance. No offense intended, understand. Just a policy of the house. You pay for your meals when you eat. You'll hear the gong when supper's ready."

A stairway reached upward steeply, and as Hilliard climbed it he moved slowly, aware of the drag of his weary muscles. As Cluny Grimes had promised, the room and the bed were neat and clean. Hilliard stacked his saddlebags, his belt, and his gun on the room's single chair, then lay back on the bed, hands clasped behind his head, a musing smile softening the hard line of his jaw.

Burnt Corral, Idaho! What had caused him to designate such a place as his home country? Idle whimsy or a touch of instinctive caution? For as Old Zeke Borders, camp cook back in the sage desert had warned, these Bannock Hills had already proven to be trouble country. So there was no telling who might be interested in him, wondering where he had really come from and why he was here. And a certain four-fingered renegade on the run would surely remember the cow town of Meridian and the robbery and fatal gunplay that had taken place there.

A partially lowered window shade shut out the full weight of the sun, and with the town now lying quiet, a restful half gloom filled the room, making it pure luxury for a man to stretch out slack and loose all over while toting up the events of the past several hours.

Hilliard pondered the possible savage consequences of the shooting of Parker Marion. He considered the foreboding expressed by Molly Clement and Hester Loring and Skeeter Dahl's gloomy forecast of bitter results and decided that he very well could have ridden into some kind of hill-country feud or range war. After all, he had been forewarned of such a possibility; Old Zeke Borders had seen to that.

Whatever the setup, there was nothing he could do about it now, so Hilliard put his mind on more pleasant things. The picture of a vivid, dark-haired girl came immediately to his mind—so straight, so haughty, so proud as she strode across the store platform, with laughter and words so bright and clear. Then came the swift and complete change of manner as the full, dark significance of the word he brought struck home. After that she had raced from town on that pretty, piebald pony!

What, he wondered as he drifted off to sleep,

would she find at the end of that furious ride? Hope or despair?

He was awakened by an insistent jabbing at his ribs. Opening his eyes, he realized that he'd slept away the balance of the day. For now lamplight spread its meager glow across the room's deep gloom. Dazed and bewildered, Jud Hilliard came up on one elbow, held there by the demanding pressure of a gun muzzle boring against him.

"Far enough!" was the harsh order. "Stay that way!"

Four men were in the room with him. One was the hotel owner, rabbit-faced Cluny Grimes, who was stuttering an anxious explanation.

"I—I don't know a thing about this f-fellow, Mr. Marion. He just said he wanted a bed for the night and maybe a couple of meals. The name he gave is on the register. I—I knew he was a stranger, but past that—well—!"

"Not blaming you, Grimes!" was the deep-voiced reply. "You just go on about your business. We'll take over here. All right, Hube—get that fellow up so we can have a good look at him and see what he has to say for himself!"

A hand dropped on Hilliard's shoulder, giving him a yank that nearly rolled him off the bed.

"All right, you! On your feet!"

Jud Hilliard stood, the hot threads of an awakening anger raveling along his nerve endings. The three remaining men were all in range clothes.

Two of them had emptied Hilliard's saddlebags under the fitful glow of a small, wall-bracket lamp. They had pawed through all his belongings, tossing aside his spare shirt and socks, his extra bandanna handkerchief, his razor, soap and brush, a double handful of .44 Colt cartridges, his sack of pipe tobacco. They had even emptied the little metal container that held his supply of sulfur matches. And they had also found the gun that belonged to the wounded rider.

"It's the kid's gun, all right, Garr," one of them said. "You figure this jingo was aiming to steal it?"

"We'll find out about that right now!"

They stood before him, all three of them. The one holding the gun on him laid out further harsh words.

"Mister, we got some questions to ask, and you damn well better have all the right answers!"

A steadily mounting tide of hot, bitter anger was surging in Jud Hilliard as he flung back his retort. "And you damn well better have some legitimate answers yourselves! Just who in hell do you think you are, invading my room, jamming a gun in my ribs, pawing through my belongings? As for any stealing going on, who gave you the right to rifle my gear? What answers have you got?"

"This," charged the one behind the gun. "This—for all of us!"

With his free hand he slapped Hilliard savagely in the face, then backhanded him as he reversed the blow. It happened too fast and violently for Jud Hilliard to see it coming or to ward it off, and the two contacts carried enough force to stagger a man. Reeling as he tried to regain his balance, Hilliard collided with the edge of the bed and fell back across it. The fellow who had hit him leered down at him.

"That answer enough for you?"

Jud Hilliard's first surge of dazed and bewildered anger had been merely hot and resentful. Now it became a wild, raging fury. Though he was flat on his back on the bed, he doubled his knees and drove both booted feet at the leering face above him. The fellow tried to jerk back and away but didn't make it fully clear, getting his face out of the way but taking the driving smash of Hilliard's feet into his chest, to send him floundering backward. Cat-fast, Hilliard was up and after him, hammering a vengeful fist home that sent him all the way down, slamming his head against the floor and jarring the gun from his hand.

Hilliard dived for the weapon, got hold of it, and was coming up and around when a man's full, crushing weight landed on his shoulders, driving him to the floor, grinding his face against the worn boards. Desperately he tried to roll and fight free, but a heavy gun barrel thudded against his head, and he lost the world in an explosion of light.

When the world returned to him, he lay on a hard wagon bed under a velvet-black night sky laced with the cold glitter of stars. His clothes clung to his chest and shoulders, wet and chilled, while his clubbed head rocked with torment at every jolting lurch of the wagon. When he tried to ease his position a little, he found that he was tied, hand and foot. This discovery renewed the numbed coals of anger to a brand-new white heat and cleared his thoughts enough to begin recalling several things; among them were some words Hester Loring had spoken.

". . . I doubt you'll be thanked for this. Far more likely you'll come to wish you'd never seen or heard of anyone named Marion!"

Abruptly the road slanted upward and the world grew darker as lofty timber closed in to shut off the starshine. Men rode beside the wagon, silent save for an occasional growled word. The road kept climbing, becoming rougher, and the misery in Hilliard's head increased to where a particularly heavy jolt sent him partway into a deep stupor.

How long this held he did not know, but when full reality returned to him, there was starlight in his face again and the air was heavy with the bovine odors of cattle close by. Here also was the damp breath of a creek, and the wagon dipped into the gurgle and splash of hurrying stream waters. Hilliard recognized the grating slide of iron tires over wet gravel, and as the wagon hauled out the far side of the stream, the scented breath of wood smoke lay across the night. Close ahead lights shone in house windows. Men gathered around the wagon as it jolted to a halt.

They cut away Hilliard's bonds and hauled him from the wagon. When he tried to stand, his knees buckled and the world turned upside down. He'd have gone over in a heap if they hadn't held him up. He fought back savagely against the weakness and nausea, and when by sheer grim power of will he managed to steady himself, he knocked their hands aside and cursed them, low and bitterly.

"Keep your damned paws off me!"

"Well, now," somebody said, jeering, "he'd still play it tough, would he? Maybe he needs another working over, Garr."

"No more of that" was the growling reply. "I'm beginning to think we've already made damn fools of ourselves. We'll take him inside, but no more rough stuff."

There were too many of them to try to resist. So Jud Hilliard let them steer him up some steps, across a wide porch, and through a door into a huge chamber of a room where the flames of pine wood leapt and crackled in a great, rock-faced fireplace.

The ceiling of the room was massively beamed. Heavy-framed, leather-covered chairs stood around, and there were three equally heavy tables, each of them holding a kerosene lamp. A wide, deep-furred bearskin rug was spread before the hearth, and in a chair beside it sat a man with a bold, dark face and a shock of hair that the hard years had turned snow white.

On his left knee a kitten dozed, purring, comforted by the touch of his hand. Resting on a low stool, his right leg was pushed straight out. It was only half a leg. From the knee down it was a peg of hickory wood, tipped with a ring of iron. On the floor beside the chair lay a crutch.

"Bring him close. I want to see what there is behind his eyes!" The man's voice was deep and resonant.

They pulled Jud Hilliard forward so that he stood before the white-haired man, there to meet the impact of a scrutiny that was as penetrating as it was stern.

"I am Caleb Marion," the man said. "I would like to know more about you, such as where you came from and why you are in this country."

Some of the heat from the hearth touched Hilliard but not enough of it to penetrate the clammy wetness of his sodden clothes. So now a violent chill gripped him, turning him weak and shivering, while again the world was tilting crazily.

"You," he said defiantly, striking back through shaking lips, "can go to hell! And I hope your son dies!"

That was all he could manage before toppling over, with the floor coming up to meet him, slamming hard against his face. He lay there, convulsed with chills and an ever-increasing tide of bitterness.

Voices clashed above him, the dominant one belonging to Caleb Marion. Grimly prepared to take further punishment, Hilliard was surprised when it did not occur. Instead he was lifted up and placed in a chair. A glass was pushed into his hand, and somebody growled a gruff order.

It was whiskey, a massive jolt of it, and when he got it down, the shock of it spread all through him. A blanket was placed around his shoulders, and between the comfort of this and the warming effect of the whiskey, the chill lessened and he quit shivering. But the misery in his head persisted, and there was something dribbling down the side of his face. When he attempted to brush this away, it left a scarlet stain on his hand. He lifted his punished head to meet Caleb Marion's bleak and demanding glance.

"Didn't mean all of that just now," Hilliard mumbled. "Not about your son dying. He never did me no hurt, so I take back that part of it. But for some others, like the one who slapped me around while holding a gun on me—and the one who gun-whipped me—well, I want another chance at that brave pair!"

Again crimson dribbled down his cheek, and again he wiped it away. Watching, Caleb Marion exclaimed harshly.

"Garr, this man is bleeding! I told you to fetch him here so that I might talk with him—but only that. Why was he mistreated in this way?"

"Because he came up tough" was the reply. "He knocked hell out of Hube."

"Without reason, you mean?"

"Not exactly" was the subdued answer. "More and more I'm realizing that we all acted like damn fools. But Hube slapped him a couple of times, which turned him wild. He crawled all over Hube and got hold of Hube's gun. No telling how things would have turned out if I hadn't laid my gun barrel across his head. I was wrong about that. We were all wrong. And I'm sorry."

"You damn well should be," growled the old man. "I'm in no way surprised at Hube starting it. He was born a fool and will no doubt die one." The hard, dark glance came back to Hilliard. "And what is your version of what happened?"

Hilliard shrugged. "I'm asleep in my hotel room. A fellow woke me up by jamming a gun in my ribs. Two others were going through my saddlebags, scattering my gear around. Naturally I objected. When I did, I was slapped down. So I went after that fellow and got his gun. Before I could use it, somebody jumped me from behind and bent a gun barrel over my head, knocking me cold. When I came out of it, I was laying in the back of a wagon, tied hand and foot, like I was some kind of damn criminal or wild animal. I was soaking wet. They must have emptied a bucket of water on me. I was brought here. That's it."

His hating glance roved the room, in turn touching each lank, dark-faced man standing there. One of them spoke.

"You had Park's gun in your saddlebag. Like maybe you were figgerin' to get away with it?"

Jud Hilliard's retort was as curt and as savage as his feelings. "Now, there is some real damn-fool talk! Or is it that this country is so full of thieves that they believe everybody's one? When I found the wounded kid, the gun lay beside him. It didn't make sense to leave it there, so I brought it along to get it back to someone who had a right to it. My big mistake was mixing in any of the affair in the first place. I was told in town I'd probably end up wishing I'd never seen or heard of anyone named Marion. How right that word!"

"Who told you that?" came back at him harshly.

Hilliard's shrug admitted nothing.

One of the dark-faced crew cursed, "Give me my way and this proud bucko will damn quick start answering questions without any more smart back talk!"

"Hube," growled Caleb Marion, "you shut up! Same applies to the rest of you. I'll do all the talking necessary."

He was turning to Hilliard again when a call came in from an outer door.

"Cody just rode in!"

The big room went still—very still and very quiet. Watching the old man before him, Jud Hilliard saw strain turn iron-hard cheeks into bitter lines. Tension piled up in the room to the point where even Hilliard himself had to hold his breath.

The scurry of quick steps sounded, and the dark-haired girl appeared before Caleb Marion.

Marion dragged a single questioning word across grim lips. "Parker...?"

"Alive, Father!" the girl burst out, the twist of piled-up emotion in her voice. "Yes, alive! Hester Loring and Molly Clement have stopped the bleeding. And because Park is young and strong and the bullet did not stop in him, Hester Loring said there is hope for him. Also, she said that if Park lives, it will be because he was found and brought to care as quickly as he was."

Some of the strain left Caleb Marion's cheeks, to be replaced by a flare of quick, stern anger.

"You hear that, Garr—and all the rest of you? If Park lives, it will be because he was found and cared for by this man. A man we have repaid by rifling his gear and clubbing him with a gun barrel when he objected. What kind of fools have I in my house?"

Garr Marion stepped forward. Tall and dark-faced, he had his father's direct eyes and sternly cast features. For a second time he voiced blunt apology.

"I said I was wrong about that. If it will do any good, I'll say it again. But the fact remains that somebody shot Park, and I intend finding out who did it, no matter what means I have to use!"

Caleb Marion nodded. "Of course. There will be no mistake about that. First, however, we repay what we can of the debt we owe this man before me. His head needs attending to. Take him where it can be done."

"Not necessary," Hilliard said curtly. "All I want is to get back to town. Past that—what any of you owe me..." He paused and looked around before adding harshly, "I'll collect in my own good time and way!"

Sternness flowed out of Caleb Marion again. "You will not leave as you are. Your head needs care, and that care will be given. Later on I would like to talk with you again."

Once fully aroused, raw anger was a consuming flame that died slow and hard in Jud Hilliard. And that flame was burning hotly, too much so to be completely allayed by any placating words.

About to repeat his demand for an immediate return to town, his swinging and still savage glance met the girl's, and in her eyes he saw clear concern and unspoken appeal. He hesitated. Why should this be? Unable to come up with a satisfactory answer, he voiced his decision.

"Fair enough. Let it be so."

It was Garr Marion who led him out of the big room into another equally large one. There was warmth from a fire in that room, and the luring odors of hot food. A long table was flanked with benches and chairs. The far end of this room was kitchen country, with a miscellany of pots and pans lining shelves and hanging on wall pegs. More of the same, simmering on a big, black iron stove, gave off gusts of savory steam. A grizzled old man in a flour-sack apron hovered over the stove, and as he caught the smell of hot coffee, Jud Hilliard realized abruptly that along with the rest of his miseries he was wolf-hungry.

Garr Marion squared a chair for him, then went over to the stove and came back with a cup of coffee.

"Maybe you could use this," he said.

"And though you can hate me clear past the hottest depths of hell if it will make you feel any better, don't hold it against the old man. Because it was like he said—all he wanted was the chance to talk to you. The rest of this stupid mess was all the fault of Hube and Wilce and myself, none of it his."

Noting the eagerness with which Hilliard drained the cup, Garr Marion nodded. "Of course, it would be so. We dragged you away from town before you'd had any supper. We'll take care of that right now!"

He called to the cook, who brought food. It was good food, piping hot and plenty of it, the first Hilliard had tasted since the frugal bite or two early that morning back at his overnight camp at the start of this eventful day. As he ate, his thoughts turned wry. Just short moments ago he'd been full of the fires of fury, prepared to hate any and all of these people, ready to strike back at them any way he could. Yet now, here he was, eating their food and liking it.

The food eased the worst of the weakness out of him and quieted the inner emotional fires, tamping down all residue of raw anger. Of half a mind to admit this, he looked up. But when his seeking glance touched Garr Marion, the considered words were unspoken.

This man, standing so straight and tall beside him, was staring into what were plainly very somber thoughts. There was a settled grimness about Garr Marion's mouth, and his eyes were hooded in a dark speculation of some kind. Here, Hilliard decided, was a strong man, but never a truly mean one. There was too much character framing that lean, dark face, too much courage burning in the dark, deep-set eyes. Any mistakes this man might make would be honest ones, honestly admitted. Also, Hilliard decided, when better known under less severe and strained circumstances, here was a man who would be easy to like and to call friend.

Done with his meal, Jud Hilliard was pondering his next move when the door of the room opened and the girl, Cody Marion, came through it. She crossed quickly to the stove, then came over beside Hilliard, bearing a basin of hot water and several towels. Warm concern shone in the clear depths of her eyes, and when Hilliard attempted to push to his feet, she spoke with an impulsive quickness.

"No, please don't get up. It is as Father said— your head must be cared for, and I can do that better while you are sitting. Also, I must thank you personally for all you did for—for Park. I—I just can't tell you how much it means to me!" Her words thickened until they were almost a sob in her throat. A swift rush of tears misted her eyes. She gulped, shook her head, and went on.

"I—I've always seen him as a—a little boy, my little brother. And now, even though he is a man grown, to me he is still my little brother and means so much—so much! And please, for how we've treated you, you must not hate us!"

There was a sweet fragrance about her, and as she worked at Hilliard's clubbed head her touch was sure, her hands slim and deft. When she finished, Hilliard came to his feet.

"All things are better now," he said gently. "I felt mighty good to hear that Park was making the grade. In fact, I had a hunch right along that he would, because a pair of good women are taking care of him, and when such a pair make up their minds to it, they can fight off the devil with their bare hands. Which is what is now happening out at the Clement ranch."

"Yes, yes!" the girl exclaimed. "You hear that, Garr? Good women, wonderful women—both of them. While we Marions have so much to be sorry for and apologize for! Things we've thought— things we've said. As though we were better, when really we're not half as good. We've been too proud—and stupid! You hear that, Garr?"

"I hear" was the grave answer. "You're right, Cody, right all the way. It's high time the Marion family changed their thinking about a great many things. At the same time," Garr added sternly, "there will be no change at all concerning who it was that shot Park. That fellow I want!" Turning to Hilliard, he spoke in a milder tone. "If you prefer things so, I'll take you right back to town. Yet I know Father would appreciate another and quieter talk with you, probably wanting the details of how you happened to find Park, who is his special favorite. This thing is riding the old man hard, and with that bad leg of his there isn't much he can do except think and wonder and ask questions. So maybe, if a talk could ease matters, well . . . ?"

Cody Marion's soft "Please!" was an echo to her brother's request.

Managing a faint smile, Jud Hilliard nodded. "Of course."

"Obliged," Garr Marion said. "Obliged for all of us."

CHAPTER
4

CALEB Marion was just as he had been when Jud Hilliard first faced him. The crippled leg rested straight out before him, and his glance was fixed with a brooding intentness on the leaping, curling flames of the fire. That glance lifted and swung as Hilliard and Garr Marion entered. There was an empty chair waiting, and Caleb Marion waved Hilliard to it while rumbling a gruff greeting.

"You are feeling better, Mr. Hilliard? And do I have your name correctly?"

"Everything is much better," Hilliard assured him. "And you do have the name right. It is

Hilliard, Judson Hilliard." Then, because of the promise he'd made to Garr Marion, and to the girl, Cody—particularly to her—Hilliard smoothed out both his thoughts and his next words. "There is something you wished to ask me about?"

"If you don't mind," the old man growled. "I have no wish to pry into your personal affairs, understand. What I'm after is any possible word or hint that might lead me to the person who shot my son and why they shot him. So I would like to know how you happened to find Parker. I need to have all that clear in my mind."

Jud Hilliard felt his damp shirt pocket and found it empty. Observing and understanding the move, Garr Marion was swift to proffer a sack of Durham tobacco and a cluster of sulfur matches. Tipping his head in thanks, Hilliard proceeded to roll and light a cigarette with slow care, using the pause to sort out his thoughts. Then he proceeded to tell how he came to find the wounded man.

Caleb Marion listened intently, his glance searching Jud Hilliard's face. He nodded. "Did you hear any shots before you found Parker's horse?"

"No," Hilliard said. "None at all. I wondered over that at first. But in backtracking the buckskin, the blood sign I followed was already mostly dry, so I figured the shooting had taken place while I was still a considerable distance back down in the timber—maybe even where I had camped. That is all broken, heavily timbered country where the sound of gunshots would not carry very far. So, no, I heard nothing and saw nothing beyond what I've told you."

Caleb Marion's glance lifted to meet that of his eldest son. "What do you think, Garr? Maybe somebody in the Wade outfit?"

Frowning, Garr Marion's reply was hesitant. "Had some thought that way at first," he confessed. "But now . . ." He shrugged and shook his head.

"I'd hate to think it, myself," the old man said, "because Sam Wade looked me square and steady in the eye when he gave me his word that the bad old days were over and done with forever. Of course, the man is a damn Yankee!"

Garr made a hard, dismissing gesture. "Which is something I'm all through holding against any man. I agree all the way with Cody that it is high time we Marions changed our thinking about a number of things, one of which is that the war you and Sam Wade knew is long over and best forgotten."

Caleb Marion grunted and changed the position of his crippled leg. "Not that easy for me to do. And if it wasn't a Wade, who else and why?"

His cigarette smoked out, Jud Hilliard tossed the butt into the fire and made quiet observation. "All this is strictly none of my business, of course. Yet I'd offer a suggestion. When I picked up Parker's gun, by force of habit I opened the loading gate and spun the cylinder. One chamber had been fired, which meant that Parker had thrown at least one shot at somebody or something. Might be good sense to wait and hope the kid recovers enough to tell about it. That way you won't be guessing and guessing wrong, as you did with me."

Garr's agreement was quick and vigorous. "Makes all kinds of good sense! We jumped in headfirst, wild and crazy, and made complete damn fools of ourselves where you were concerned. So from now on it's going to be different. And besides, Cody is dead right. For much too long we Marions have been plenty wrong about certain people, looking down on them, even sneering at them. At one in particular. Yet if Park lives through this, that one person is one of those we can thank for the kid's life."

Caleb Marion again stirred restlessly. "You'd be speaking of the Loring woman, of course?"

Garr tipped his head in a nod. "And as Cody says, how can we ever thank her enough?"

Again Caleb Marion grunted. "Don't forget your pride. Man without pride ain't even half a man."

"That all depends," Garr retorted. "Too much of the wrong kind of pride can make a fool of a man and rob him of many of the better things of life."

Growling, the old man waved an irritated hand. "Let it be." He turned to Hilliard. "My thanks for bearing with me. Now Garr will take you back to town. As you suggest, we'll wait until Parker is able to tell his side of the affair."

Before stepping out into the night, Garr Marion held a fleece-lined coat for Jud Hilliard to slide into. Men were gathered around a waiting wagon, and as Hilliard and Garr Marion approached, a low growl of voices quieted until someone dropped a curt, harsh question.

"The old man satisfied with him?"

"Of course," answered Garr tersely. "We all are."

"Not all—not me" came the bleak retort. "I still ain't trustin' him none."

"You wouldn't, of course," Garr shot back. "Best thing you can do, Hube, is shut up! You never did talk good sense!"

Climbing into the wagon, Jud Hilliard pulled the borrowed coat snug around his shoulders. Overhead, the dark vault of the night sky was all awash with stars that laid a frosty glint across this mountain world, filling it with a thin and biting chill.

For a short distance the wagon rolled a fairly even way before tipping downslope to splash through hurrying creek waters. After that came extensive meadowland where cattle shifted on either side, their stirring shapes burly in the starshine. Next there came the filtered gloom of timber country. The ride was made in silence until Jud Hilliard commented dryly, "Got to admit that this is a lot more comfortable ride than it was coming out of town. And I'm enjoying it more."

Beside him, Garr Marion shifted restlessly and softly swore. "I've been mentally booting hell out of myself ever since. Real truth is, even on the way out to the ranch I was anything but proud. Goes to show what a jackass a man can make of himself when he lets his emotions get the best of his common sense. And I can't rightly blame you if you're set to hate the entire Marion family."

Hilliard chuckled softly. "Not that bad, man— not that bad at all. And while I think of it, here is something else. The empty saddle that buckskin horse carried was a high-class-looking kak. In my judgment, strictly first-quality stuff and entirely too good to be left out there any longer than necessary. Because when the buzzards and the coyotes start working on the carcass of the horse, they could damage some high-grade saddle leather."

Garr Marion was quick to agree. "That saddle was just about Park's dearest possession. The kid was pure miser with his money for a long, long time, saving enough to buy the rig. Practically had it made to order. I know I'm not deserving of a favor from you, but how's for directions so I can locate the buckskin?"

"Pretty thick country thereabouts," Jud Hilliard recalled. "Be much simpler and easier if I was to ride out with you."

Garr made harsh exclamation. "Man, more and more you shame me! But if you would...?"

"Tomorrow morning," Hilliard directed. "Better bring along an extra horse to carry the saddle. Also, while we're there we can cast around some and maybe stumble on some lead that would help find an answer to the big question of who—and why."

"I'll be in to buy breakfast for both of us," Garr agreed. He paused slightly before going on, and when he did, he picked his words with a slow care.

"Seeing that we're sort of laying things on the line, I'd like to make a try at explaining why the Marion family went off so wild and stupid. Cody said it all when she thanked you. To all of us Park has been the kid brother, the one we'd watched grow up from a little fellow. And just like it was with the old man, we all felt extra-special about him. In consequence, when the word came that he'd been shot, we all went out of our heads and started hitting wild and crazy in all directions. At the moment you were the only target available, and we made blasted fools of ourselves." Garr shrugged, sighed, and went on somewhat wearily. "Is that as stupid and mealy-mouthed as it sounds?"

"Not at all," Hilliard assured him. "In fact, when I came down out of my own first blaze of anger and started thinking straight, I understood your feelings. In your boots I'd have felt the same. So, as far as I'm concerned, that part of the affair is a closed book. Providing, of course," he ended wryly, "Hube leaves it closed."

"Which he'd damned well better do!" rapped Garr flatly. "I'll see to that."

Town was quiet when they rode in. Garr hauled up in front of the hotel and led the way inside. Cluny Grimes had just finished sweeping out the hotel barroom and was about to close up for the night. The sight of Jud Hilliard and Garr Marion striding in shoulder-to-shoulder made Cluny Grimes's attempted greeting a blurted incoherence. His likeness to a startled rabbit became doubly apparent.

Garr Marion's instructions were brief and crisp. "Earlier this evening, Grimes, several people made sad fools of themselves. I was the biggest fool of the lot. But all that is past. From now on you're to give this man your best attention and service." So saying, Garr put a steady glance on Hilliard and offered an outstretched hand. "A privilege, if you will?"

Jud Hilliard shook hands heartily. "Of course. See you in the morning."

Garr Marion turned and left, a tall, erect figure. Cluny Grimes watched his departure anxiously before turning to Hilliard, pointed nose twitching, eyes even more protuberant than usual. It was as though he'd just witnessed something he hadn't believed possible.

"I had no part or meant anything during that earlier affair in your room, sir. It was just—just—"

"Sure," cut in Hilliard, smiling to himself. "I understand. So now, with everything squared away, how about getting me back in my room?"

Reaching for his keys, Cluny Grimes headed for the stairs. "Right away, sir. You'll find things exactly as they were left. I locked the door. Garr—Mr. Marion—ordered me to do that."

Climbing the stairs, Jud wondered at the sudden steepness of them and the effort it took to mount them. He decided it must have been a rougher night than he'd realized. One that had taken a lot out of him. That waiting bed would be plenty welcome....

Cluny Grimes put a match to the wall-bracket lamp, and the light showed Hilliard that everything was about as he recalled before the world went away from him under the clubbing impact of Garr Marion's gun barrel. The contents of his saddlebags were spread around, but as far as he could see, nothing had been taken, not even his gun. So even as he wielded that clubbing gun barrel Garr Marion must have had some misgivings.

Cluny Grimes made a few quick passes at smoothing out the bed before retreating to the door where he hovered anxiously. "Anything more I can do, sir? If there is anything you want, just yell."

Now Hilliard grinned openly at him. "Fair enough. But next time, should somebody come looking for me, see that I'm awake and prepared for company before you let them in."

Cluny Grimes flitted away like a frightened ghost, his hasty words trailing behind him. "Have no further worries, sir. And about things earlier this night, I'm sorry—mighty sorry!"

Jud Hilliard wasted no time in shedding his clothes, putting out the light, and climbing into the blankets. He straightened out with a long sigh of relief. His clubbed head, though still sore, no longer ached, while the tension that had tied him up inside now eased away.

He pondered drowsily as to how and why it all had come about. How, he thought, brooding, could a man be savagely furious one moment because of a deep injustice and only a short time later become, if not entirely forgiving, at least knowing an increasing tolerance and understanding toward those responsible for the injustice? When and why had this change of heart come about?

He finally decided that it was when Cody Marion had come in out of a tense and tortured night with word of her kid brother's condition. It was startling how clearly he recalled those bitter moments. When word came that the girl had just ridden in from the Clement ranch, the big room had gone utterly still and been charged with a strain so deep and vital that even he, though still convulsed with savage anger, had virtually held his breath. The expression on old Caleb Marion's harsh and brooding face had turned iron hard as he waited.

And then came the bursting relief that followed when the girl, in a rush of tears, gave out her message of hope.

That, Hilliard realized, had to be the moment when the change in his feelings had occurred. For here lay proof that these people, rough though they had been with him, were as warm and humanely concerned among themselves as any ordinary, close-knit family would be. And for that reason the family could not be too bitterly blamed for a mistake made under the pressure of grief-scrambled sentiments.

Jud Hilliard's next thought returned to the bleak and sworn purpose that had brought him into this hill country in the first place. His was an odyssey of vengeance, this relentless search for a certain four-fingered man. Hilliard realized that his quest, once of such all-consuming purpose, had been momentarily blunted and pushed aside by unrelated happenings closer at hand.

Long miles back in a wide, sagebrush desert, Old Zeke had warned him about the Bannock Hills. Trouble country it had been called, and trouble country it had certainly proven to be. He was mixing in deeper with some of that trouble. And in the morning he would return to where an unfortunate saddle pony had died and where its young rider, shot through and through, had lain so close to death. Hilliard had done his best to give that young rider a fair chance at life. What more, if anything, did he owe to the Marion clan? Maybe the really smart thing for him to do would be to get out very early in the morning, saddle up the big red horse, and head out far and fast from these Bannock Hills.

It was a thought he discarded almost before it was fully formed. Because only a few minutes ago he had sealed an agreement to meet a man, come tomorrow morning. And, Hilliard reflected, you didn't go against your word.

Beyond the open window of his room, night's quiet lay full and deep, spreading a chill breath across the world. Jud Hilliard settled farther under his blankets and welcomed the onrush of sleep. And the final picture that formed in his mind before full sleep took over was of a slim girl with tear-wet eyes, bringing a message of hope into a room where waited a grizzled, iron-faced old soldier.

CHAPTER
5

THE morning stars, though still high in the sky, were beginning to lose their brilliance before a steadily increasing flow of dawn fire streaming in across the eastern hill crests. Morning air pouring through Jud Hilliard's open window was thin and biting cold. Responding to its brisk urging, Hilliard rose early and looked down on a street that lay empty and silent, held in deep shadow.

He had lived so long with the single thought of vengeance that it had pushed all other thoughts aside. His obsession with vengeance had made him somewhat emotionally stodgy and unresponsive. However, over the short space of twenty four hours, he now found himself cast into a new role and held by new interests.

In the semidarkness of his room he washed up and felt his way into his clothes. He went downstairs to find both the hotel and town silent and empty. He had the street to himself and went along it to the stable where Skeeter Dahl, lantern in hand, was starting his morning chores.

"What's the idea, you up and rustlin' around this early?" said Skeeter. "By all rights, after what happened last night, you should be set for at least a week in bed!"

Hilliard shrugged. "Nothing that bad. Where did you get the word?"

"Cluny Grimes," Skeeter Dahl said. "After the Marions hauled you away last night, Cluny was so full of excited gossip, he acted like he wasn't sure whether he was here or somewhere off yonder. What set the Marion crowd after you, anyhow?"

Hilliard shrugged again. "A little misunderstanding that's all straightened out now. How's that horse of mine doing?"

"Ready to go. You taking him out today?"

"Right after breakfast."

Back in the depths of the stable a soft whinny sounded. Skeeter Dahl exclaimed, "That's him now. Heard your voice and wantin' to say good mornin' to the boss. Smart rascal that one. Let's go see him."

The light of Skeeter's lantern led them through the stable gloom to a box stall where a big red horse hung an anxious head over the side. He nuzzled Jud Hilliard's shoulder as Hilliard gently mauled the big fellow's head and ears.

"Kinda fond of him, ain't you?" Skeeter observed.

"Kinda," Hilliard agreed. "We've been traveling together for quite some time, Red and me."

"Sure is a lot of bronc," Skeeter said. "And there's somethin' I been wonderin' about. That little line of white hair low down on his off shoulder. What's it from, a snag scar?"

"No," Hilliard said. "From a Sioux bullet."

Skeeter's eyes popped. "A Sioux bullet! How come?"

"Red and I went up the valley of the Little Bighorn together," explained Hilliard tersely. "We had a lot of luck, so we came out of it together. And when we got back to Fort Lincoln, where the quartermaster sergeant was a good friend of mine, he arranged things so Red and I were mustered out together."

"Be damned!" Skeeter sputtered. "Should have guessed something of the sort, for you've the cavalry look about you—way you pack your shoulders and such. Well, I'll have the big fellow ready to go when you want him. Now—other things to do."

He led the way back to a street that was no longer empty. Up at the hotel Garr Marion had just pulled it at the hitch rail with an extra horse at lead. He was out of the saddle when Jud Hilliard reached him. He looked at Hilliard out of tired eyes. An edge of the same weariness was in his voice.

"Didn't expect to find you up this early. Personally I got damn little sleep, being all stirred up with worry about Park. But I'm ready now for hot coffee and all the other breakfast fixings." Garr's glance ran over the dark and silent hotel, and there was an impatient growl that harshened his next words. "That Cluny Grimes—he can be a lazy little badger. Let's go roust him out and start him busy in his kitchen."

"Not necessary." The turning of Jud Hilliard's head indicated Hester Loring's little eating house, where a light now burned. "Seems open for business."

Garr Marion hesitated before speaking slowly. "Doubt I'd be welcome in there."

"Not welcome! Public eating house, isn't it?"

"Depends. Maybe not if that public is a Marion," Garr pointed out soberly. He considered a moment before shrugging. "Still might be worth a try. Abner Roblin can't do any worse than run me out." He led his horses over to the place, tethered them, and followed Hilliard inside.

It was a modest little layout with a short stretch of counter, fronted by half a dozen tall stools. Beyond the counter a big black cast-iron stove creaked with heat. On it a coffeepot steamed, and an open oven door disclosed a pan of fresh-baked biscuits. Just turning away from the stove was a grizzled old man, sleeves rolled to his elbows. At the sight of Garr Marion he went very still, staring, before laying out a flat statement.

"This I never expected to see—not you in here. Can't say I like it, either."

"Understand your feelings perfectly, Abner," returned Garr quietly. "But a number of things have changed since yesterday. I'd appreciate a breakfast for my friend and myself."

"Your friend!" the man exclaimed. "After all the rough stuff that went on last night, this friend stuff is a little hard to swallow!"

"That," explained Garr patiently, "is one of the things that has changed. So now—how about some breakfast?"

Abner Roblin shrugged. "Fair enough. Guess it'll be all right. Feeding you, I mean. Miss Hester never said I couldn't. So, what'll you have?"

"Anything that is quick and hot."

The food was both. Sizzling ham steaks, fried

potatoes, biscuits with wild honey, and copious coffee. Abner Roblin placed the coffeepot handy to their reach, then turned back to an inner door.

"Got to get Terry up and feed him too. Be back right away."

Jud Hilliard's glance followed Abner Roblin. "I like that old codger. I like anybody who is faithful to a trust."

"Just so." Garr nodded. "Ab will do to take along."

They were busy over their plates when the outer door swung open, letting in another customer. It was Nile Starkey, the man who had been with Cody Marion when Hilliard rode into town with his somber message.

"Damned lazy little polecat!" Starkey said of Cluny Grimes. "Wasn't even stirring when I got up. If he's going to run a hotel, why doesn't he attend to business?"

He broke off abruptly as the significance of Jud Hilliard and Garr Marion sitting amicably side by side struck home. "Considering the happenings of yesterday and last night—in particular last night—this I can't figure!" he said.

"Don't try," Garr Marion told him tersely. "Seems everybody is wondering. Call it that a bad mistake has been corrected and that a number of things are different than they were. What brings you up and around this early?"

Nile Starkey shrugged heavy shoulders. "Edgy, restless, I guess. Stewing about Parker and trying to sort out some kind of answers that make sense. What's the latest word about Park?"

"Last night, encouraging," Garr reported. "I'll know more as soon as I can get out to the Clement ranch."

"Any idea yet on who might have pulled the trigger?" queried Starkey. "You think maybe one of the Wade crowd?"

"Dangerous talk, dangerous thinking, so quit it," charged Garr quickly, words and manner curt. "I'm blaming nobody for anything, until I know a lot more about everything." He tipped a nod toward Hilliard. "You fellows have met?"

"We've met!" Hilliard was blunt about it. "And considering some of the remarks made, I have to wonder a little at his being here."

Garr's head swung around. "Remarks? What kind of remarks?"

Before Hilliard could answer, the rear door of the room opened and let in Abner Roblin, shepherding carefully the small boy Hilliard had seen with Hester Loring. "Grab a stool, Terry," the old man directed. "I'll have your breakfast mush ready in a jiffy."

The boy scampered around the end of the counter and was eyeing the loft of a stool with some uncertainty when Garr Marion lowered a big arm, looped it about the little fellow, and lifted him up. "Right here, Terry—right next to me."

In the next breath it was Abner Roblin laying a harsh challenge across the room. "Starkey, what are you doing in here?"

Nile Starkey's reply held a clear edge of hesitation that he tried to cover up with a show of bluffed heartiness. "Why, ah, looking for some breakfast, of course, Ab. Coming by, I smelled good food cooking and thought—"

"Get out!" cut in Abner Roblin savagely. "Get out! You've been told before that you'd never be welcome in this house. Now you're being told again—and for the last time. You hear me? Get out!"

Startled, Jud Hilliard watched raw anger convulse Nile Starkey's face, his eyes narrowing to moiling glints, the outthrust of his broad and heavy jaw becoming more pronounced. When Starkey answered, his words were eruptive, thick, and ugly.

"Why, you damned old fool—who do you think you're talking to? That's no way to speak to a customer. I've a notion to—"

"Get out!" cut in Abner Roblin remorselessly. "Ain't tellin' you again. I'll get my gun!"

The old fellow was swiftly up to the counter and reaching under it when Garr Marion spoke. "Won't be necessary, Ab. He's leaving."

Suddenly bleak, Garr's glance raked Starkey. "Guess that's it, Nile. You better drift."

Starkey swung a hand across in front of him with a hard, slashing vehemence. "No, by God!" he exploded. "Damned if I will! If you can eat in here, I can. Tell that old fool so!"

Garr Marion laid aside knife and fork, spun around, and stood up. "I told you to drift, Nile. Right now Abner Roblin is in charge of this place, and when he says you're not welcome here, that's good enough for me. So you're leaving—now!"

Nile Starkey's burning, furious glance locked with Garr Marion's cool, level one, and the cool, level one carried the most weight. Nile Starkey was up on his toes, chest swelling as though challenging combat. But the challenge ended there. With another slashing hand swing, Starkey whirled and stamped out.

Turning back to his seat, Garr Marion again slid an arm around the little lad next to him and spoke with a quick comfort. "All right, Terry, now that that's been taken care of, we can get on with our breakfasts. Hot mush coming up for you."

During the brief moments of strain as tides of hostile emotions charged the room, the boy's eyes had grown big and round and touched with uneasiness. Now, with Garr's reassuring tone and manner, plus the solid, protective comfort of his big arm, the boy relaxed and leaned even closer inside the strong circle of that arm.

Observing these reactions, Ab Roblin's murmur was full of outright wonder. "Never saw the little feller friend up so quick and complete with a stranger before," said the old man, his careful glance searching Garr's face. Gruffly he added, "Obliged, of course, you sidin' me against Starkey, though just why you did puzzles me a mite. Must be like you say about things being different, for when I tie this and that of just now with other things that have happened in the last day or so, then I got to admit that things sure are different!"

Garr's answering smile was brief and slightly grim-lipped. "Just water down the creek, Ab—that's all. Now, how's for Terry's breakfast?"

Done with their food, Hilliard and Garr Marion twisted up smokes and returned to the street, which still lay empty save for Garr's two horses. In the hotel, lights, pale and furtive in the quickening surge of the new day, now burned. It was a fact that Jud Hilliard remarked on.

"Somebody must have dragged Cluny Grimes out of the blankets. Starkey, you think?"

"Probably." Garr nodded. "And if you're wondering about me going raunchy with Starkey, I'm halfway wondering myself. But all of a sudden, for some damn sudden reason, I found I'd had plenty of Nile Starkey. Maybe it was because of the way Ab Roblin tore into him. Ab never would have gone that hostile without some good reason. Then there was something you said when I spoke of you and Starkey having met before. You made mention of some remarks that could have held more than they should. Perhaps a sneer?"

"Yes," Hilliard said. "A sneer."

"Why, then," Garr declared crisply, "I'm glad I took the rawhide to him."

"Starkey?" asked Hilliard. "What's his stake around here? A ranch, maybe?"

Garr shook his head. "Cattle buyer. Works out of Keystone. Seems to know his business. Got a reputation as a shrewd bargainer. Well, now for the Clement ranch. And I'm holding my breath, wondering."

As Skeeter Dahl had promised, the big red horse was saddled and ready to go. Being well rested and fed, it was eager to run a little too. But Hilliard held the big fellow back to the more sedate pace of Garr Marion's pair.

Out ahead the valley was all awash with early morning's lingering mists, deep and shadowy blue against the timber on either side, but thinning to a building glow where quickening daylight gilded the valley center. The air was keen and sweet with the many fragrances of space. It was a pretty morning in pretty country, and Jud Hilliard remarked on the fact.

Garr Marion grunted. "Never was anything wrong with the country. It's the damn stupidity of the people in it that makes for trouble."

Hilliard's head swung as his glance picked up movement at the edge of the timber.

"Speaking of people," he said, "here comes one of the better members!"

"Hell! It's Cody!" Garr exclaimed. "Independent as a jaybird on a high limb, and as usual, going her own way. I told her to stay home and rest up—that I'd bring the latest word on Park's condition. Might have known she'd do as she damn well pleased!"

She came out of the shadows, her little calico pony cantering easily along a trail that curved in to meet with the valley road. She brought her pony in beside them and spoke quickly against Garr's questioning glance.

"Don't scold, big brother! I just had to see for myself how Park is doing. On top of that I want to be useful. I doubt that Hester Loring and Molly Clement got any rest last night. So it is only right and fair that I do what I can to see that they get some rest today."

Eyeing her fondly, Garr nodded. "Of course. And, as usual, completely right."

Her glance lifted to Jud Hilliard. "And you, Mr. Hilliard, how are you? Your head—your other hurts?"

"Couldn't be better—and forgotten," he assured her, smiling.

He thought of her as she had appeared while crossing the store platform with Nile Starkey: a strikingly handsome young woman, moving with something very close to haughty arrogance.

Now here she was, appealingly young and girlish as she rode beside him. He smiled down at her, and as she met his glance a little stain of color touched her wan cheeks. She covered this with some exclaiming words.

"My, that horse of yours certainly is big, Jud Hilliard. On this little pony of mine I feel dwarfed beside you. What a beautiful one that big fellow is!"

"All of that, for a fact," Hilliard agreed. "And if for some reason you ever happen to be up on old Red and wanting to go someplace in a real hurry, you'd need only to shake the reins and tell him to go. You'd think you were riding the wind."

She turned again to her brother Garr. "You sent Pete Shields to Keystone after a doctor. How long before they can get here?"

"Hard telling," Garr answered soberly. "If Pete's lucky enough to locate a doctor who is free and willing to make the trip, they might get here sometime late tonight—or tomorrow morning." Brooding for a moment, Garr added grimly, "Park's got to make the tough part of this ride in the hands of Hester Loring and Molly Clement."

The sun broke clear of the timber tops and laid its full, warm glow over the entire valley as they turned in at the Clement ranch. A grizzled ranch hand watched them come up. Cody Marion was out of her saddle swiftly. Glimpsing the straining demand in her glance, the old rider nodded reassuringly.

"He's hanging on as well as can be expected, missy. Tough young cub, that boy!"

"Thanks, Boley," the girl said fervently. "I'll probably be here all day, so you better take the saddle off Patches." She tossed the reins to him and hurried into the house.

Now it was Garr Marion who stepped down and put his glance on the old ranch hand. "My turn to say thanks, Boley. You've been helping all along the line, so I'll get back at you somehow."

Stripping the saddle off the calico, Boley Oakes paused, shrugging gruffly. "What the hell! Just been actin' the decent human being is all. Besides, I'm some fond of the kid, as he allus has a good word for old Boley." Speaking, Boley got out his pipe and began packing it. "No idee yet who threw that slug into Park?"

"Nothing that makes sense, but sure looking for something that does." Garr tipped an indicating head. "Meet Jud Hilliard. He's the one who found Park."

Boley Oakes lifted a callused finger in salute. "My pleasure, friend. Accordin' to Miss Loring and Mrs. Clement, the main reason the kid is alive right now was your findin' him and rustlin' help the way you did."

Hilliard nodded acknowledgment.

There was movement at the ranch-house door, and Cody Marion hurried out, sending her call ahead. "You'll have to saddle Patches again, Boley. I've got to go back to town after some things Hester Loring needs. Or maybe, Garr, I should take your horse?"

"Not necessary," Jud Hilliard said quickly. "Take old Red, here. All morning he's been fretting to run, which he loves to do. Take him. It will do him good."

Speaking, Hilliard began shortening his stir-rups. Cody Marion came up beside him, hesitant but eager. "Do you think I could stay with him? He stands so big and powerful."

Hilliard smiled. "Of course you can stay with him. As I said before, you'll think you're riding a smooth wind. Now, up you go!"

Speaking, he cupped his hands and, when she put a slim, booted foot into them, tossed her lightly into the saddle. For a moment he mauled the horse's head and ears gently. "All right, you big tramp. Be a real gentleman and take good care of the lady." Hilliard looked up at the girl. "Just lean a little forward and shake the reins. Red will do all the rest."

Cody Marion reined the big horse down to the main valley road at an easy pace. But once she reached the road, she turned him into it and let him go.

Watching, Garr Marion said, "She looks so small up on that one."

Boley Oakes nodded. "Like a little kid. But she can ride, that girl can. And man—look at that bronc eat up the distance!"

Jud Hilliard grinned. "After hauling me around Red will figure he's running under an empty saddle. He'll have the lady to town and back before the little calico would be even halfway there."

Again there was movement at the ranch-house door, and this time it was Hester Loring who stepped out, spreading her arms to greet the sun. Garr Marion moved swiftly to face her, hat in hand as he searched for the proper words to express his feelings.

"Been wanting this chance, Hester—so I could thank you personally."

She stiffened, and her answer came sharply. "It is always Miss Loring to you, sir. You should know that."

Garr tried again. "I—we Marions—are all very grateful—"

Again she cut him off. "I neither want, need, or expect thanks from any Marion. In particular from you or that bitter old pirate who is your father. What I've done, and will continue to do, is for a badly wounded boy and for his sister, neither of whom are as yet fatally infected with that dark and vicious thing you older Marions choose to call your pride."

Watching and listening, there was, Jud Hilliard realized, something more behind this exchange than showed on the surface. Hester Loring was slicing Garr Marion to ribbons, and clearly he was near on his knees to her.

"Very well, Hester," said Garr defiantly. "And yes, I will call you Hester. The pride you correctly named as a dark and vicious thing no longer exists. The Marions are in deep debt to you. And even though you refuse to accept our thanks, you must consider them tendered. Now I would even ask a further favor of you. What is your latest word on the chances of my younger brother, Parker?"

For a little time she gave no answer, just holding Garr's demanding glance with that steady defiance.

"He lives," she said curtly. "That is all. But he has gone far down into the pit, so about all we can do is hope."

"Isn't there even a glimmer of light?" Garr persisted.

Again considering Garr Marion intently, Hester Loring nodded. "Yes, there is that glimmer."

Listening, Jud Hilliard sensed a slight softening in her tone.

Garr Marion bowed his head. "Thank you, Hester Loring."

After which he turned away and headed back toward the corrals where Boley Oakes was taking care of Cody Marion's little calico pony. Moving to follow, Jud Hilliard had one more look at the strong, handsome woman standing beside the ranch-house door. He saw that her glance was now following Garr Marion and that the defiant severity of her expression was no longer there, replaced now with a faint and gentle smile.

CHAPTER
6

IN the town of Willow Creek, Nile Starkey
was in a foul state of mind. The bluntly
hostile reception he'd met with from fiery old
Abner Roblin, together with Garr Marion's stern
backing of the old fellow's stand, taunted him.
And though the breakfast he'd finally managed
to stir up at the hotel had been well cooked and
plentiful, Starkey had found little satisfaction in
it, while his surly mood left Cluny Grimes wondering and worried.

Done with the meal, Starkey sought a chair on
the hotel porch where the morning's sun spread
a warming glow. He brought out a cigar, gnawed

the tip off it with a wrenching twist of heavy teeth, lit up, and, through a bloom of smoke, surveyed the empty street with a scowling glance. He was still there, brooding over his sour thoughts, when he heard the mutter of speeding hoofs. Soon a slim, bare-headed girl on a big red horse raced into town and pulled up in front of Hester Loring's eating house.

Cody Marion was out of the saddle quickly, pausing only long enough to run a caressing hand along the neck of her mount before scurrying into the house. Held momentarily with a startled stare, Nile Starkey pushed to his feet and strode over to the horse. He was there when Cody Marion reappeared, carrying a small, well-wrapped bundle.

"Nile!" she exclaimed. "How lucky! Because you're able to reach much higher than I can, and so tie this bundle behind the saddle for me. This horse—so big, so powerful! And how he can run!"

Her hair had been loosened during her ride, so that it was fluffed around her face, framing cheeks that had been wan and drawn from a long night of worry and very little rest. Now her cheeks were faintly brushed with color, and there was a quickening shine in her eyes.

Nile Starkey made the requested bundle tie but took his time doing it. "How's it happen you're riding this horse? What's wrong with your little calico bronc?"

"Not a thing wrong with Patches," Cody told him. "But Hester Loring needed these things in a hurry, and Jud Hilliard offered the loan of big Red so I could make better time. And Jud surely was right when he said it would be like riding the wind!" Speaking, Cody jumped, caught the saddle horn in both hands, and lithely pulled herself up far enough to scramble into the saddle.

"Well, well," Starkey drawled, his tone thinly dry. "So it has already become Jud, has it? I'd say that's moving pretty fast for a drifter neither you or anyone else in these parts knows a damn thing about. I doubt your father would approve."

Cody looked down at him, a quick spirit flashing in her eyes. "Now," she told him curtly, "you're talking like an idiot. All that counts are the things in this bundle, needful for the care of my brother Parker. Let's go, Red—take me back!"

The big horse came around so sharp and fast that a driving shoulder clipped Starkey, staggering him. Then Red was away and racing, Cody Marion crouched low in the saddle. She did not look back.

Fighting to regain his balance, Nile Starkey spilled a current of startled curses, growling his open anger as he stared after her.

"There are times, young lady, when you get a little too proud!"

Starkey made another survey of the street to see if the incident had been observed by anyone else. Satisfied that it hadn't, he headed for the Gilt Edge bar.

Out at the Clement ranch they watched Cody and her mount come storming back along the valley road.

"That big, red son of a gun is travelin' just as fast comin' as he did goin'!" Boley Oakes exclaimed.

"Of course," Jud Hilliard agreed. "And so far he's just been enjoying himself."

Leaving the valley road, Cody Marion came on up to the ranch buildings at an easier pace. When the big red trampled to a halt, she twisted in the saddle, untied her bundle from behind the cantle, and handed it down to Boley Oakes. "Hold this a minute, Boley."

Standing at her stirrup, Jud Hilliard showed her a small smile. "Quick trip, wasn't it? Has Red been a gentleman?"

"He's wonderful!" Cody declared fervently. "And I love him. On Patches I'm always so close to the ground. On this fellow I'm in the clouds."

"In which case," Hilliard suggested, "you could probably accept a hand down?"

When she did come down, it was with a rush

that Hilliard slowed with a ready and encircling arm. Cody faced him breathlessly, her eyes big and startled. Then she slipped away, reclaimed her bundle from Boley Oakes, and quickly went into the ranch house.

Looking depressed and whipped down, Garr Marion came over from the corrals, leading his pair of horses. He spoke slowly as he watched Jud Hilliard adjust the stirrup length again.

"Now that you've got your horse back, maybe we can get along after Parker's saddle gear?"

"Right with you," Hilliard agreed, toeing his stirrup and swinging up.

Garr led the way down to the valley road where Hilliard pulled even with him, though keeping his silence, well aware that Garr was worried about his brother Parker's condition and bruised by the scalding going-over he'd taken from Hester Loring. So they covered some little distance before Garr straightened up, gave his shoulders a loosening shake, and spoke.

"You know, Jud, there seems to be a fundamental balance of justice that's bound to catch up with a man and exact full payment for whatever brand of damn foolishness he's been guilty of in the past. Now, even if that is as mealymouthed as it sounds, it still sure as hell applies to me."

Hilliard's understanding grin was small and contained. "Could be. But personally I go for the idea that it's more important generally how a man faces up to and finishes a tough chore than how he starts one."

Musing on this as they climbed the switchback grade into the timber, Garr nodded. "Makes sense. Kind of comforting too."

Jud Hilliard needed no roadside checkpoints to recall the exact spot where a desperately wounded young rider had lain sprawled the day before. That picture was still too sharp and distinct in his mind's eye. Reining up, he pointed.

"Right there, Garr. That's where I found your brother Parker."

A ragged spread of dark crust stained the thin dust of the road, with a scatter of green flies hovering over it. Impulse pulled Hilliard out of his saddle to break up and wipe out the crust with a scuffing boot toe.

Back in his saddle, Hilliard spurred his horse forward. "Now we'll go get Park's gear."

Perched in a tree overlooking the little clearing below the road, a lone buzzard craned a naked head as they approached, then lurched away in somber, heavy flight. As yet, however, neither winged nor four-footed scavengers of carrion had really gone to work on the carcass of the luckless buckskin horse.

Shaking out his rope, Jud Hilliard dropped a loop around an outstretched, death-stiffened rear leg, threw a dally, and put the big red to a pull that turned the carcass over far enough for Garr Marion to loosen the latigo tie, drag the saddle clear, and remove the braided rawhide head stall. Garr loose-cinched the gear on the spare horse he'd brought along. Then he put a last sober glance on the buckskin.

"A mighty good little bronc, that one was, and Park's favorite. The sight of it makes me want to come up with the miserable whelp responsible for all this. Let's see what we can do toward running down some kind of convincing answer."

"If there is such an answer," Hilliard said with a nod, "it would have to be somewhere up around the road where the shooting took place."

They climbed back up the slope, and as they reached the road, Garr quickly pushed ahead, growling swift warning across his shoulder.

"Watch it, Jud—watch it! That's Sam Wade out there!"

Reared high and alert in his saddle, Garr sternly eyed the approach of a rider who came steadily toward them.

"Steady, Garr—steady!" Wade yelled as he reined his horse. "No reason for you to get your roach up and look at me that way. Can't you get one big truth straight in your mind, once and for all? There's not a trace of the old, blind idiocy left in any member of the Wade family. All of which I told your father some time back!"

Sam Wade was tall, rawboned, and sandy-haired.

He had a solid jaw, and his blue-eyed glance was steady and direct. "Truth is, I was on my way to face either you or your father and talk over a couple of things that have me wondering. But we'll get to that later. Right now, and much more important, what's the word on Park? How's the boy doing—how's he making it?"

Garr hesitated, reluctant to answer. Wade was impatient. "Man, what does it take to make you understand?" he said harshly. "Can't you get it through your head that all the Wade family are honestly concerned about that boy? We see him as a real fine lad and are all fond of him. In particular there's Sally, my girl. Park has been visiting with her regularly, and the two of them hit it off real friendly. Fine young people, those two kids, and much too smart to waste their lives hating and quarreling. So, may God forever damn whoever it was that pulled the trigger on that boy! Now, once more—and this time give me a decent answer. How is Park?"

Settling back in his saddle, Garr spoke carefully. "Facing a mighty tough ride but with things looking a little better this morning. He's at Molly Clement's place with Molly and Hester Loring and his sister, Cody, looking after him. I've sent outside for a doctor. And, Sam—meet Jud Hilliard, who found Park and brought him to care."

Sam Wade ducked an acknowledging head. "My privilege."

Bringing his glance back to Garr, Sam Wade's expression brightened as he exclaimed his honest pleasure. "Now, that's mighty good word about Park and will sure be welcome to all the Wades— and to Sally in particular. The girl's been fair out of her mind ever since we got first word about the boy."

Bringing out his smoking, Garr began spinning up a cigarette. "How did you get the word, Sam?"

"Billy Janes brought it from town last night along with some grub items from the store." Wade looked over the lead horse and the gear it carried. "That's Park's kak, of course. Everybody envied the boy that rig."

"Hilliard and I just collected it," Garr explained. "Now we figure to scout around and search for some kind of sign that could point a finger."

"Where was it you found Parker?" Wade asked Hilliard.

"Down road a little way from here."

Sam Wade frowned for a moment before looking back uphill. "Has to be some real reason for the shooting," he observed soberly. "Shootings don't just happen without cause or purpose. And just for instance, up yonder a little this side of the Dorcass trail turnoff, there's a sign where maybe half a dozen head of cattle crossed the road in the past day or so. Of course, this may not necessarily mean a thing. Then again," Sam Wade added significantly, "maybe it could. I'd say it is worth another look, anyhow, to sort of line up where the stock could have come from and where they were heading. Let's go have that look."

Sam Wade started to rein his horse around, but Garr Marion stopped him with a quick remark. "Obliged for the word, Sam, but no need of you bothering further. This whole affair is strictly a Marion concern, and we Marions will settle it."

Rising impatience burned in Sam Wade's blue eyes and charged his tone with harshness. "Man, quit being so damn proud! Maybe it is mainly a Marion concern, but there's an angle you've yet to hear about that makes it a Wade concern too. None of my people shot your brother. But somebody did, and whoever it was, for some shifty reason of their own, could be figuring to try to lay the blame on me and mine. So shuck that cussed, stiff-necked Marion pride for a change, and open up your thoughts a little!"

Silent so far, but missing nothing, and aware of the gathering tension, Jud Hilliard said, "Garr, I thought we agreed last night that you'd never be entirely certain of anything unless and until your brother Park recovers enough to tell his own story. That made sense then, and it makes sense now. I'm remembering that Park's gun had one fired shell in it, which means that Park got off a shot himself, and I'm wondering at who or what—and why. As I see it, Sam Wade, here, is being smart and reasonable all the way, so it would pay you to listen to him."

Nodding wearily, Garr pushed a hand across his face and eased back in his saddle, his words slightly muffled as he spoke. "Of course, he's right. Sorry, Sam, for being so thickheaded. But ever since the word of the shooting reached me, and with the worry over Park piling up, my thinking has been clumsy and stupid."

Sam Wade nodded in understanding. "Hell, man! It's easy to see how that would be. So now let's go at this thing together."

They rode up to where the cattle had crossed. After looking over the sign Garr Marion agreed with Sam Wade's findings.

"Half a dozen head would be about right," he said, "with three riders hazing them. But who would be doing that at this time of the year? None of the Marion family that I know of."

Sam Wade had dug a stubby, badly charred pipe from a pocket and now, while loading and lighting it, was held in frowning thought. Through the first good, blooming cloud of tobacco smoke he studied Garr Marion intently. Abruptly he nodded, as though having arrived at some satisfactory decision. Now he spoke with slow, measured care.

"I wouldn't know who was driving them, but if I had to make a guess at where the cattle came from, I'd have to say it was from the Grizzly Flats range where you and your people have been running the only pure Durham stuff in these parts. No, I wouldn't know who was driving them, but I do know where that little jag of Durham young stuff is right now. Garr, those critters are feeding on Wade grass in Cache Valley—I was on my way to Marion headquarters to report this to either you or your father."

Garr's face flushed with anger at the seeming accusation.

"Easy, man—easy! I'm not accusing you or anybody else of anything. I'm just laying out the facts of what I've seen with my own eyes."

Once again the silent, judging observer, Jud Hilliard saw in Garr Marion and Sam Wade two basically sound men, both honestly intent on moving well away from the animosities that once had existed. Hilliard realized he was in a position to mediate.

"Though a stranger hereabouts and on short acquaintances with its affairs, I've a thought I'd like to get off my chest." He twisted in his saddle to face Sam Wade.

"Only minutes ago, Mr. Wade, you mentioned the possibility of someone trying to point a finger your way by putting Marion cattle on a part of your range. Can either you or Garr think of anyone who might profit by getting the Wades and the Marions at each other's throats again?"

Sucking on a pipe that had begun to fry, Sam Wade's eyes pinched down. He shook his head with a slow gravity. "Not right off, I can't. But, friend, that brings up something that can sure stand some thinking about. When I backtracked that little gather of Durham young stuff from my Cache Valley range to this road, the closest headquarters I passed along the way was the Dorcass place. Didn't see anybody around just then, but it might be a good idea to give that headquarters a more direct visit right now. What do you think, Garr?"

There was a definite emphasis in Garr Marion's quick nod of agreement.

"Hell, yes, Sam! Both you and Jud are thinking way out ahead of me. Let's go see if we can stir up Elgie and Duff Dorcass and ask some damn well-pointed questions!"

They went back along the trail Sam Wade had used in tracking the stock. It led through an area of low, timbered ridges and small, shallow valleys, one of which held the Dorcass headquarters. It was a shiftless-looking layout, the buildings drab and weather-beaten, the sprawling corrals carelessly laid out. There was no sign of life.

Garr Marion headed right up to the ranch house. He swung down and thumped a heavy fist on the door, which swung open slightly. Getting no response, he pushed the door wide and stepped through. Quickly he reappeared, grim-faced as he beckoned Jud Hilliard and Sam Wade from their saddles. Sam sent a question out ahead.

"Something wrong, Garr?"

"Come see!" was Garr's brief reply.

The interior of the house was just as worn and shiftless as the outside. Daylight peered furtively through windows long unwashed and now scummed with dust and cobwebs. The whole place was foul with stale human odors. Sam Wade looked around, then exclaimed in disgust, his lip curling.

"Damn hog pen! Smells like one too!"

Garr indicated the ragged shred of towel that hung on the back of a rickety chair. "What do you make of that, Sam?"

Sam Wade moved closer, had his look, then came sharply around. "Hell, man—those are bloodstains on that rag!"

"What I figured," Garr agreed. He turned to Jud Hilliard. "How do you see it, Jud?"

"Same as Sam," Hilliard answered soberly. "And I'm remembering that Park's gun showed he'd thrown at least one shot at somebody or something."

"Just so," rapped Garr harshly. "Now we look a little farther."

An adjoining room held two bunks heaped

with untidy tangles of musty blankets. More ominous stains on one of these stirred another exclamation by Garr.

"Like you said, Jud, the kid got off one shot, and by the looks of things here, he didn't miss!"

Sam Wade cut an angry hand across in front of him." Damn affair gets dirtier and dirtier. Leaves a man up in the air, wondering where to turn and what to expect next." He looked at Hilliard. "Would you have any more ideas, friend?"

Hilliard answered with slow care as he stared ahead, sober conjecture. "Let's go back to where the shooting took place. Sam, both you and Garr agreed that the trail sign showed three riders were driving the cattle. From what we've been looking at here, it's fair to assume that two of the riders were the Dorcass brothers. And I'm wondering who the third rider might have been. At a guess, maybe somebody Parker would know and who didn't want to be known. And desperate enough over it to try to kill the boy? I admit I'm just reaching here and there with my thoughts. But for what they are worth, what do you think of them?"

"Man, you're beginning to scare hell out of me," Garr said bleakly. "Damn such thoughts! But keep on with them, because they make sense. What else do they tell you?"

"For one thing, there's this angle," Hilliard offered. "Earlier today, Sam, here, suggested the possibility of someone deliberately out to stir up the old trouble between the Wades and the Marions. And I see it as mighty important that you two squelch that possibility as quickly as you can. By being seen publicly, shoulder to shoulder in open friendliness, preferably in town, so the word could travel fast and far."

"I like that idea," enthused Sam Wade. "I like it plenty. How about it, Garr—how about right now—today? With us standing right up to the bar in Buck Saddler's Gilt Edge bar, having a couple of drinks together? And I'll buy the drinks!"

"Let's ride," Garr said, heading for the outdoors. "After seeing this mess, a jolt or two of Buck Saddler's bourbon should help clear the air."

They returned to the switchback grade and down to the reach of the main valley road. When they came even with the Clement ranch turnoff, Garr's face went stern and set as he murmured his thoughts aloud.

"Stay with us, Parker, boy—stay with us!"

Town was quiet as they hauled up at the Gilt Edge hitch rail. Another horse under empty saddle stood at tie there. Garr's nod indicated it.

"Seems some other Marion is in town. That roan is Hube's favorite bronc."

Buck Saddler was a short, broad man with an amiable moonface. He was behind the bar, leaning across it to watch Nile Starkey and Hube

Marion shake poker dice. At the moment Hube Marion had the dice, and he was talking to them as he pounded the leather cup on the bar top. But at sight of the three men who entered he went still, the cup half lifted.

Lining up at the bar with Garr and Jud Hilliard, Sam Wade called for a round of drinks.

"Make it the best you have in the house, Buck. And I'm buying."

"With the next round on me," Garr proclaimed.

Staring, Hube Marion rapped out a harsh question. "What the hell is this, Garr? Some sort of celebration?"

"Call it so," Garr told him. "Just celebrating the return to common sense."

"Common sense, hell!" Hube blurted. "Don't make a lick of sense to me. And I don't like what I see—not a little bit, I don't! Those you're with—what about them?"

"Well, what about them?" was Garr's curt return. "Two of the finest men I know."

"Not to me, they ain't," proclaimed Hube heavily. He turned to Starkey while shaking up the dice. "This is my last roll, Nile, then I'm headin' out. I don't care for some of the just-arrived company."

He flipped the leather cup, sent the dice tumbling. He read them at a glance, then returned them to the cup.

Watching, listening, it was Jud Hilliard's turn

to go very still for a moment before carefully pulling his glance away.

Because the left hand Hube Marion used in scooping up the dice had only four fingers on it.

The middle finger was missing!

C H A P T E R
7

OUT at the Clement ranch, Boley Oakes welcomed two new arrivals. The first of these was a sturdy, red-cheeked, fair-haired girl. Boley's greeting was gruff but kindly.

"You," he said, "would be Sally Wade?"

"Yes," she told him, a small break of emotion in her voice. "I—I want to know about Parker Marion. How is he?"

"From all reports, coming along first-class," Boley assured her. "Stout young cub, that boy. And getting the best of nursing care."

Watching, Boley saw some of the strain and tautness of worry lessen in the girl's face, saw her soft lips tremble and tears of relief mist a pair of blue eyes.

"I—I want to help care for him," she said, faltering. "Do you think I might?"

Boley reached for her rein. "Ain't a single good reason why you shouldn't, youngster," he told her gently. "You go on in. I'll take care of your horse."

Quick to alight from her saddle, Sally Wade crossed to the ranch-house door. It was Cody Marion who answered her knock. Cody exclaimed softly.

"Sally—Sally Wade! And like the rest of us, of course, concerned about Parker?"

Again the glint of tears misted Sally's eyes. "I want to help, any way I can. Even—even if I could just sit beside him."

Cody held out impulsive hands. "Of course, of course. Come on in. Though there isn't too much more any of us can do until the doctor gets here. They—Hester Loring and Molly Clement—have been wonderful, for they've stopped the bleeding, which is all-important right now. Yes, come on in!"

At first glance the two older women understood and made room for Sally Wade at the bedside of the long, lean young rider who lay so very still, his youthful face drawn and pallid. At first sight of him Sally Wade began to whimper like a hurt child. Hester Loring dropped a comforting hand on her shoulder and spoke softly.

"If you watch closely, my dear, you can see that he's breathing steadily and well. I have a strong feeling of hope in this."

Reaching up, Sally caught hold of Hester Loring's gentle hand and pressed it to her cheek.

The next arrival at the Clement ranch came in by buckboard in the first blue gloom of early dusk. Dr. Phineas Craig was a tall, gaunt man with tired but whimsical eyes. As he climbed stiffly down from the buckboard seat, professional satchel in hand, he laid that whimsical glance on the young ranch hand who had driven him all the way from Keystone and spoke in a singularly deep, rich voice.

"Long haul, wasn't it, son? Let's hope it wasn't in vain." He turned to Boley Oakes, who had moved in through evening's deepening shadow.

"The patient, how is he?"

"Still with us, Doc," Boley affirmed. "And, they tell me, more than holding his own. Some mighty fine womenfolk in there, nursin' him."

"Ah, yes, and wonderful," approved Dr. Craig. "It is ever a comfort at a time like this to have such women on hand. They always supply just the proper touch."

Again it was Cody Marion who answered the door, and it was her turn to have misty eyes as she exclaimed.

"Dr. Craig! Welcome—welcome!"

She led him into the sickroom where he boomed a brisk, "Good evening, ladies all! I sense an atmosphere here that is very encouraging. But I want a glance or two at the patient before I scrub up and get to work."

Such glances were steady and intent. Then Dr. Craig nodded his approval. "Plenty of life still in that boy."

He scrubbed up in the ranch kitchen, opened his satchel, and got to work, murmuring his thoughts in medical terms as he progressed with various basic tests. Finished, he straightened and looked around.

"Good ladies, I congratulate you and stand amazed. Both entrance and exit wounds clean, sterile, and properly bandaged. A touch of fever, of course, and to be expected. Past that, and barring any unforeseen complications, it is my full judgment that the biggest problem ahead for this lad is that he get back some of the blood that he lost. To that end he must have complete rest, proper nourishment, and this continued fine nursing care. Ah, the magic of youth's deep strength together with a heritage of clean blood! There is no substitute for such.

"And now," he went on, "as I remarked to the ranch hand who drove me here, it was a long, long haul from Keystone. So now I wonder if there be in this hospitable dwelling a chance cup or two of hot coffee together with a well-covered plate of food for a very hungry man...?"

Immediately Molly Clement was scurrying around, exclaiming her apologies before heading toward the kitchen. "Oh, Doctor, I'm so sorry. I just wasn't thinking. And, of course, you'll be staying the night?"

"That," proclaimed Dr. Craig, "would be well—and what I planned on."

Busily cleaning up odds and ends, Hester Loring now spoke quietly. "You being close at hand, Doctor, means I can return to my own family in town for the night. But I'll be back in the morning, just in case."

"I'll take this good word about Park's condition to my father and others of the family at home," Cody Marion said.

"And I'll do the same for my people," Sally Wade said. "They're all very concerned."

So it was that old Boley Oakes, out under the early stars, had a busy few minutes, hitching the team to the livery rig Hester Loring had driven from town and saddling up for Cody Marion and Sally Wade.

About then Sam Wade rode up.

"Boley," he said, "I've the feeling I've a daughter hereabouts to squire home?"

"Right enough, Sam," Boley told him. "Just finished saddling her bronc. She's been here all day, helpin' where she could. But now, with Doc

Craig stayin' for the night, all the womenfolk are gettin' a break."

"What's Doc got to say about the boy?"

"Nothin' but good," informed Boley with obvious satisfaction. "So me, I'm plumb pleased with everything."

Shortly after, Boley was alone in the ranch yard. Hester Loring had already driven away in her buckboard, and Cody Marion was on her way home. Now Sam and Sally Wade rode off.

Beginning to feel the full weight of his years, Boley tramped wearily around to the back door of the ranch house and, as was usually the case, ate his supper in the kitchen. Finished with this, he headed directly for his cabin bunkhouse and the blankets awaiting him there. At the bunkhouse door Boley paused, looking and listening alertly, not at all certain but that he'd sensed the presence of something or someone over by the feed sheds and corrals. For a minute he watched and listened carefully but found nothing more than night's full stillness and silence. So he shrugged away the moment of uneasiness while mumbling his thoughts.

"All these damn goings-on have me a little spooky," he decided. "I'm beginnin' to hear and see things that just ain't there!"

The Clement ranch house was a sturdy, spacious building, boasting a neat little dining room that was Molly Clement's special pride. In the comfort of the room, Dr. Phineas Craig relaxed and ate a bountiful supper, paying his hostess the supreme compliment of accepting a second helping of everything. Finally replete, then delving a pocket for a well-used pipe, he rumbled whimsical thanks in his deepest tones.

"With your permission, Molly Clement," he added. "I go now for a quiet smoke under the stars. Which will comfort and sustain me for the long night-watch ahead."

The stars were there, all right, in their full, chilling brilliance, silvering a vast and silent world, save for the far-distant yammer of a coyote, early on the hunt. However, in some degree starlight could prove treacherous, for in contrast here and there, it created pockets of deep shadow. And from one such shadow a half-crouched figure closed in behind Dr. Craig's unsuspecting back.

While casually sauntering across the area between the ranch corrals, a cloud of pipe smoke wreathed about his head, Dr. Craig became abruptly aware of a presence behind him. Before he could turn, he felt a hard point of contact between his shoulders, followed by muffled words.

"Easy does it, Doc. That's the muzzle of a gun you feel—and don't make me use that gun! Don't yell or raise any fuss. You and me are taking a walk across the upper meadow into the timber.

Behave yourself and do as you're told and you ain't got a thing to worry about. Move out!"

Being neither a coward nor a fool, Dr. Craig did as he was told, and not until he and the man with the gun reached the timber and moved into it did he speak his first words.

"If it's money you're after, friend, you're out of luck. For I haven't a thin dime in my pockets just now. What I had is back in the ranch house with my satchel and gear."

"Not your money I'm interested in" was the answer. "It's the savvy you pack between your ears that I have need for. Just keep moving. I'll steer you where I want you to go."

They climbed a low ridge and dropped down into a small clearing beyond. Here a couple of horses began blowing and stirring uneasily. Here, also, was a blanket-wrapped figure lying inert against the earth.

"All right, Doc—that there's my brother Duff. He's been packing lead and losin' a lot of blood. So you get busy and do what you can for him."

Dr. Craig cleared his throat. "How can I do anything without light of some sort? I must be able to see if I'm to do any good."

"I'll make light," said the man with the gun. "I'll build a fire. While I'm doin' it, you stay put. I'll be watchin' you—plenty!"

Dr. Craig waited, not too sure that this wasn't all some sort of nightmare. He was near to pinching himself to make sure this was actually reality.

Dr. Craig heard the crackle of dry brush being gathered, broken, and stacked. Presently a furtive, uncertain blaze rose up.

"All right," said the man with the gun. "Now you see how old Duff is doing!"

Dr. Craig knelt beside the blanketed figure. As he peeled back the blanket the odors that came up to him told him much—told him everything, in fact. For they were stale and chilling odors. Dr. Craig explored with quick, expert hands. The man with the gun stood behind him, leaning and exclaiming urgently.

"All right, Doc—what you goin' to do?"

Dr. Phineas Craig got back to his feet, drew a deep breath, and stood very straight, tensing himself for most anything. When he spoke, it was with a flat, stern emphasis.

"There isn't anything I can do," he said steadily, "because this man is dead!"

"Dead!" The word was almost a blurting cry, and the muzzle of a gun was again a jamming thrust against him. "That can't be! Not old Duff... dead! Doc, you're lyin'—you know you're lyin'! I've a notion to—" The words rang out as the pressure of the gun muzzle increased.

"It would do neither you nor him any good if you were to kill me," Doc Craig said evenly. "And I'm not lying. I never lie about such things. I'm sorry to have to say this, but that man there is most thoroughly dead!"

Again came the blurting cry, this time unintelligible. The pressure of the gun muzzle fell away. And the words that followed were wailing and near choked.

"Get out of here—out of here...! You can find your way back. Leave me and Duff alone...! Old Duff... dead—and gone!"

Dr. Phineas Craig wasted no time. He worked his way clear of the timber fringe and went down across the sloping meadow. Out there ahead, lamplight beamed warm and welcoming in the windows of Molly Clement's ranch house.

The doctor dug his pipe from his pocket. It was cold now, but he didn't mind. With the pipe clenched solidly between his teeth he felt his sense of reality return to him.

His step was steady as he entered the house.

CHAPTER
8

IN the velvet gloom of early night two men labored. One was going over his thoughts in the quiet of his hotel room; the other worked by lantern light in the heavy timber of the hills where a blown-down ancient sugar pine lay, the victim of some earlier wild windstorm. Where the spread of the uptorn roots had been was now a sprawling, ragged-sided hole in the forest floor. Here, with brooding care, Elgie Dorcass laid out the blanket-wrapped body of his brother, Duff, and began wielding a rusty shovel. As he toiled in the lantern's fitful glow Elgie spoke the words of a bitter requiem.

"Doin' the best I can for you, Duff. When I heard that Garr Marion had sent outside for a doctor, and not knowin' much about such things myself, I kept watch, and when I had the chance, I brought that doctor feller out to look at you, so I'd know for plumb sure just how it was. Doc said you were sure enough dead—so now I got to do this, and it's bustin' me all up inside!"

Pausing to move his lantern to another spot, Elgie renewed his mumbled grief. "I'm not goin' back to the home place, Duff. It never was much, and now, without you, it ain't nothin'. But I sure aim to call a showdown with the feller who talked us into this mess. I'm sure enough goin' to have a showdown with that one!"

In his hotel room Jud Hilliard was battling his own punishing thoughts. The trail of vengeance he'd set for himself had led him far, deep into this wild hill country. And here, where least expected, he'd come up with the sought-for answer. Here, beyond any doubt, he'd found the four-fingered man who had robbed and killed Pop Worley!

Hube Marion! Earlier, Hilliard mused, when he, Garr Marion, and Sam Wade stood together at the Gilt Edge bar, Hube Marion had made his show of violent hate before storming out of the place. Garr Marion's following glance had been a bleak one, and his stern words were a rueful apology to Hilliard and Sam Wade.

"That fellow is speaking just for himself, not for the rest of the Marions. Let me put it this way. As a cousin, Hube's been of the family but never truly in it. He has never truly gotten along with the rest of us, and there's been times when my deep-down feeling has been that he really hated the rest of us. Neither Cody nor Parker have ever had any real use for him. Maybe because as the youngest members of the family they knew a kind of idealism that pointed them away from him, and it could be he's sensed this and that it's part of the reason he acts like he does. Hell, there's been times when he'd haul out and we wouldn't see him for months at a time. Not very long ago he got back from one of those wild sojurns. Never would say anything about where he'd been or why he left in the first place. A strange one, Hube is, one I don't know exactly how to handle...."

As Hilliard turned Garr's words over and over in his thoughts, he reached for a decision on just what to do about Hube Marion.

Why, hell! That same, betraying, four-fingered left hand had been the very one that had cuffed him across the face that first night when the Marions invaded this very room, blindly raging over the shooting of Parker.

It was easy enough to understand why he'd failed to note that missing finger then. He'd been awakened from a sound sleep with a gun muzzle jamming at his ribs in a room charged with threat and confusion. He had had no time to note any details before being knocked cold with a clubbing gun barrel.

The fact that all this was part of a misunderstanding now genuinely regretted by the Marions offered only temporary relief, for Hube Marion was most certainly the man he'd sworn to trail down and kill. And though Zeke Borders had warned against such vengeance, what other answer was there?

Whipped by such restless, nagging thoughts, Jud Hilliard moved to the window of his room and looked out and down across the darkened town to glimpse one set of windows still aglow with lamplight—those of Hester Loring's little eating house. Hilliard realized that he'd had no supper and that some of this nagging unrest was simply the demand of honest hunger. Hoping he wouldn't be too late, he caught up his hat and was quickly in the empty street.

In the Elite, old Ab Roblin was fussing about the stove and at Hilliard's entrance came around growling protest until he saw who this late customer was. Then he mellowed.

"Was about to close up, but if it's a bait of grub you're after, I can still manage."

"Sorry to be this late, Ab, but I really am hungry," Hilliard told him.

Ab reached for the coffeepot. "Cup of this will tie you together while I put on a steak."

The inner door opened, and Hester Loring came in. Ab Roblin protested quickly. "Don't you try to do a single thing, Miss Hester. You get your rest."

She shook her head. "Not just yet, Ab. First I've got to unwind a little, though I will have some of that coffee."

She poured it for herself and brought it around to take a stool beside Hilliard. There were shadows of weariness around her eyes, but her shoulders were erect and her head still held high. She showed him a direct, measuring glance before she spoke.

"You are, of course, the principal reason Parker Marion is still alive, and according to Dr. Craig's flat opinion, with more than an even chance at complete recovery. Your finding the boy and getting him to proper care so quickly is all that saved him."

"Not mentioning, of course, the good women who took over so capably," Hilliard returned.

Hester Loring shrugged. "Molly Clement and I were secondary. You are the central figure."

"My part was all pure happenstance," Hilliard protested. "And after stumbling across the boy, how could I have done any less than I did? Certainly anyone else would have done as much."

"I wonder," she said slowly. "Don't be too sure

of that. In these hills there are some who might have sneaked off and left the boy to die. Not all people are overly fond of the Marion family and the dark, savage pride that bitter old devil Caleb Marion is always prating about. For that matter, considering the way you were treated the other night, I wonder at you not being quite disenchanted. Yet out at Molly Clement's place you seemed on the best of terms with—with Garr Marion. And that fact puzzles me."

Her slight hesitation at mentioning Garr Marion's name put a glint of amusement in Jud Hilliard's glance. "It shouldn't puzzle you," he said defending himself. "For I've found Garr Marion to be a mighty fine man—one I feel it a privilege to know and rate as a friend. The happenings of the other night that you mention rate as an understandable mistake, all circumstances considered. A mistake honestly admitted and deeply regretted by all responsible. That is," he added, "with the possible exception of Hube Marion."

"Of course, of course!" Hester Loring exclaimed quickly. "All except Hube Marion!" Her lips twisted in an expression of disgust. "That's another thing I find difficult to understand about the Marion family—how they can even tolerate that fellow around, as plainly he's an out-and-out renegade. Must be some more of Caleb Marion's so-sacred pride, I suppose."

She mused over this statement while sipping

at her coffee. Then the severity about her lips softened and became a faint smile. "You have, you know, one real outspoken champion in the Marion family—Cody. You rate quite highly with that young lady."

Hilliard grinned. "Could be that my horse, Big Red, enters the picture there. After riding him to town and back on that errand for you, the young lady didn't want to let go of him."

Again Hester Loring showed that faint smile as she nodded. "Being now thoroughly humbled by some of the harsh realities of life, Cody shapes up as a really sweet youngster. And a scared one too. Not a trace of the old swagger and arrogance left. So I'm finding it easy to become really fond of both her and Sally Wade. It is so good to see the pair of them warmly friendly in a common cause. Someone should remind Caleb Marion of that fact."

Ab Roblin put Hilliard's supper in front of him. Thanking him, Hilliard added, "How's Terry, the little fellow, making out, Ab? Probably all settled for the night?"

It was Hester Loring who answered. "I tucked him in just before coming out here. Small, active boys need plenty of rest."

"Just so," Hilliard agreed. "He and Garr Marion sure hit it off good together at breakfast, didn't they, Ab?"

"Sure did," Ab agreed, throwing a careful glance

at Hester Loring. "Like I said at the time, I never saw him friend up to anybody so quick and complete as he did to Garr when Garr hoisted him up on the stool alongside him."

Hester Loring's shoulders stiffened. "Ab, have you been keeping something from me?"

The old fellow shrugged. "Figgered to tell you all about it later. And you never did say I couldn't feed Garr anytime he wanted grub."

"No," she admitted slowly, "I never did. But this about him and—and Terry, eating together...I don't understand."

"Simple enough," explained Ab stoutly. "The boy's breakfast mush was ready, and he had to eat somewhere. So why not in here? And when Garr lifted him up alongside him, then everybody was happy." Ab paused, then added, "That is, everybody *was* happy until that feller Nile Starkey come bustin' in and goin' plenty raunchy when I told him to get out. Thought for a minute I'd need my gun to handle him. Then Garr bought in, backin' my hand and sendin' Starkey on his way. Which made everybody happy again."

Sitting quite still and silent through a considerable pause, Hester Loring turned to Jud Hilliard. "You were present? You saw and heard all this?"

Hilliard tipped a nod. "With everything exactly as Ab says."

"But about—about Garr Marion. He had no

right to run anybody—" She stammered to a stop.

"Speaking personal, what Garr did suited me just fine," Ab said defending him. "Because if he hadn't moved in, I'd've had to throw my gun on Starkey. And you wouldn't have wanted that, would you?"

She flared slightly. "Of course not! But with Terry there... a little fellow like him, seeing and hearing men quarreling... How it must have frightened him!"

Ab Roblin chuckled. "Didn't seem to. Fact is, I think he liked it. He sure friended up with Garr afterward."

"Thereby showing what a smart little cuss he is," Hilliard put in.

Shoulders swinging restlessly, Hester Loring got to her feet and moved to the inner door, there pausing to look back. Deepened color washed through her cheeks, but a small, guarded smile hovered around her lips.

"You men... all of you!"

Hilliard grinned. "Ornery critters, for a fact. And again stating that Garr Marion is a stand-up, foursquare one of us."

"You would, of course, keep saying that!" As she turned away, closing the door firmly behind her, the small, guarded smile still pulled at her lips.

Fixing Jud Hilliard with a challenging glance,

Ab Roblin laid his next words out bluntly. "There goes a great lady...and a damned courageous one!"

"That we sure agree on," Hilliard said.

Swabbing up the last of the steak juice with half a dough-god biscuit, he washed it down with the balance of his coffee. He got out his pipe, packed and lighted it, and surveyed Ab Roblin through a bloom of smoke while laying out payment for the meal.

"Obliged again, Ab, for putting up with me this late at night. I'll be around for breakfast in the morning."

Ab waved a hand. "Early or late, folks like you are always welcome."

Outside, the town lay dark and quiet, the street empty. Hilliard picked his way through the chill gloom to the hotel, there climbing to his room to seek the comfort of his blankets. Reaching for sleep, he had no immediate success, as his own problem had him by the throat, holding him in deep uncertainty.

He'd finally come up with the renegade thief and killer for whom he had searched so long and hard, only to find him a member of a family he'd come to admire and whose friendship was important to him. In light of this, should he now carry out his vow of vengeance?

It was a problem needing some stern and solid

thinking. When he finally fell asleep, he was still thinking on it.

Dawn light, peering across his room, woke him. A glance from the window showed that Ab Roblin was already on the job, and lights were burning in Hester Loring's eating house. Dressing quickly, Hilliard washed up and went down. Another diner in search of breakfast was already at the counter. It was Skeeter Dahl. He swung around, fixing Hilliard with a demanding glance.

"When you aiming to ride again, friend? That bronc of yours is plumb restless for action. I got him in my best box stall, and he's bumping around in there, wanting out. That big feller was never meant to spend much time loafin'. He wants to go!"

Hilliard grinned. "Him and me both, Skeeter. Which we will, soon as I finish breakfast."

"Go where?" Skeeter asked, jaybird-curious.

Hilliard shrugged. "Most anywhere—just to be out and moving. Probably drop in at the Clement ranch to see how Park Marion is doing, now that a doctor is on the job."

Ab Roblin put a plate of bacon and eggs in front of Hilliard and poured more coffee. "Miss Hester says Doc Craig is feeling better all the time about the boy's good chances. And me, speaking personal, I'm hoping that whoever it was shot him is frying right now in the hottest corner of hell!"

To this Skeeter nodded vigorous assent. "And should Miss Hester aim to go out to the Clement ranch again today, I'll have a rig ready for her." He turned to Hilliard. "Soon as I've grubbed, I'll saddle the big horse for you, friend."

Hilliard waved the little livery owner back to his seat. "Stay put. I'll take care of old Red."

An eager whinny welcomed Hilliard into the stable gloom, and the usual morning greeting between horse and owner took place, with Hilliard fondly mauling the big fellow's head and ears before saddling up. Once out in the street he let Red take him out of town with a first rush of speed before reining down to a jog as he moved into the long run of the valley.

It was a clear, fresh morning, drenched with the piny breath of the timbered hills around, and Hilliard savored all these fine flavors thankfully before dropping back into the dark preoccupation of his own ever-pressing problem.

Coming even with the Clement ranch gate, he turned in, and as he rode up to the ranch buildings, it was old Boley Oakes who came forward to meet him. And Boley had a rifle across his arm.

Hilliard's nod indicated the weapon. "Expecting trouble of some sort, Boley?"

The grizzled ranch hand shrugged. "Damned if I know what to expect. Things are gettin' plumb spooky around here because of people prowlin' in the dark. Like last night when I bumped right into one. But he was gone before I could get a real good look at him. Oh, I might try a guess about that, but it wouldn't make no sense, nohow."

"What's wrong with a guess, Boley?"

"Folks would swear I was goin' loco in my old age."

"Not necessarily," Hilliard said encouragingly. "Try it on me."

Boley stacked his rifle against a corner of the bunkhouse, got out a rancid old pipe, stoked it, and lit up. "A'right," he mumbled through a mouthful of smoke. "Supposin' I was to tell you that I could have swore that feller was Hube Marion. Would that make any sense to you?"

Hilliard went high and straight in his saddle, his eyes pinching down with thought. "It might," he said slowly. "Yes, it might."

"Not to me," Boley declared. "No, sir—not any. If'n he was wantin' to find out how things were goin' with Park, wouldn't he've just plain asked right out about it instead of sneakin' around like a sheep-killin' coyote? Damn funny business, if'n you ask me. Well, I can tell him one thing. He or anybody else comes prowlin' around again, they could end up arguin' with my old Winchester. But now I got chores to do." Boley wheeled away and headed for the corrals.

Over at the ranch house a screen door slammed, and it was Cody Marion who showed, hurrying toward Hilliard, words tumbling ahead of her, words nearly tearful with urgency.

"Jud—Jud Hilliard! Oh, I've been so wanting to see you—talk with you! Because I need help and advice from someone besides Father or Garr or Wilce. And I don't dare tell them—I don't dare! Because if I did, what might happen could be terrible!" Her words peaked into a small wailing cry.

Glimpsing the storm of feeling in her expression, Hilliard stepped from his saddle. Quickly she was close to him, clinging to him. He caught her by the shoulders, turning her to face him fully.

"What is it, girl, what is it? Don't tell me that after everything we've lost Parker?"

She shook her head quickly. "No, no—nothing like that! Park is doing fine—doing so well that last night he even spoke to me when we were alone. Sally Wade had gone home for the night, and Dr. Craig had to get some rest after a very long day. So I sat with Park. All at once I realized that his eyes were open and his lips were moving. He was whispering something, and I leaned close so I could hear. And it was a terrible thing that he told me!"

She choked up a little, and Hilliard waited, steadying her. She was, he thought, like a frightened child, seeking comfort. Her head was bowed against him, and presently further muffled words came up.

"Park—Park told me who shot him and how it happened. There were three of them driving some of our cattle. The Dorcass brothers and—and Hube Marion. The minute they saw Park, they started shooting. Duff Dorcass shot Park's horse and—and it—it was Park's own cousin Hube Marion who shot him! Oh, Jud, could you believe such a thing—for Hube to shoot his own—his own cousin?" Again she choked up.

"Yes," Hilliard said quietly. "All things considered, I can believe almost anything about Hube Marion."

She gave way to a small fierceness. "Hube—I've always hated him, relative or not. Somehow to me he's never been a real member of our family. Always there's been a sort of sneakiness, a surly meanness about him. I tell you, I've hated him—and I know that Park has felt the same way. But—but, Jud, what can I do about it now?"

"Don't try to do anything," Hilliard told her steadily. "Just leave Hube up to me. What you've told me makes up my mind fully about several things."

Very gently he put her aside, smiling down at her. "Sure is good to know Park is coming along so well. Now you run along back inside and keep on taking such good care of Park."

Jealous for attention, Red nickered plaintively and rubbed a velvet nose against her shoulder until she reached up to pet him.

"You see," Hilliard said, "he's telling you not to worry—that he and I will take care of things. And now we better get at it." He toed his stirrup and swung up.

Watching until Hilliard turned along the valley road toward town, Cody scurried back into the ranch house and found Dr. Craig sharing coffee with Molly Clement. To Cody's questioning glance he answered cheerfully.

"Just made a quick check and found the patient very definitely on the mend. That, my dear, is youth for you—youth with all its matchless vitality and strength."

"Then," exclaimed Cody breathlessly, "I can now ride home with that word for Father and Garr and the rest?"

Dr. Craig nodded. "By all means."

Reaching town, Jud Hilliard pulled in at the livery barn and found Skeeter Dahl hippity-hopping about, cleaning a box stall and spreading fresh bedding straw.

Skeeter flung an eager question. "What's the latest with Park Marion? You hear anything new?"

"Nothing but the best," he said. "Still a plenty weak boy, naturally, but surely on the mend. And now you better grain Red, as I could be riding again, later on. By chance, would you know if Hube Marion is in town?"

While taking over the reins Skeeter eyed Hilliard carefully. "Saw him and Nile Starkey go into Buck Saddler's Gilt Edge bar just a little bit ago." Ever jaybird-curious, Skeeter added, "What would you be wantin' of Hube?"

"To remind him of something he owes me," Hilliard supplied briefly.

Grim purpose moved with Jud Hilliard as he moved across a street peacefully quiet at the moment. Watching after him, Skeeter Dahl knew some uneasy thoughts and murmured some of them half aloud.

"That feller Hilliard is sure packin' a mean look. Sure as hell somethin' is due to bust loose. In which case, Dahl, the smart thing for you to do is to stay right here and mind your own business, complete!"

There was no hesitation on Jud Hilliard's part. He knew what he was going to do—what he had to do! He had known these things the moment Cody Marion, standing tearful in the circle of his arms, gave out the true facts surrounding the shooting of Parker Marion. And, too, he understood her fears of carrying the words to her father and to Garr. In particular to Garr, who was certain to call Hube to account, and perhaps, hesitating at throwing a gun on Hube, so become still another victim....

Such was Jud Hilliard's reasoning as he stepped through the door of the Gilt Edge barroom, a wire-thin edge of alertness honing his nerve endings.

Hube Marion and Nile Starkey were nursing drinks and trading idle talk with Buck Saddler. But at Hilliard's entrance Hube Marion came quickly around, a hot malevolence congesting his glance. And immediately he mouthed a heavy, challenging demand.

"Mister, what the hell business you got in here? You're no way welcome!"

There was no hint of amusement in the slight smile Hilliard showed him. Only the bleak chill of ice, as was the tone of the blunt words that followed.

"There's something I want to remark on—something I intend to deliver and to collect for."

As Jud Hilliard came deeper into the room, he swung a little wide so that he would have Hube increasingly in the clear before him while laying out his harsh message.

"The name of the town was Meridian. Yeah, Meridian—just a quiet little country town, made up of the best of people. In particular there was old Pop Worley, who owned the general store. No kinder, gentler man ever lived than Pop Worley. I know, because he was my foster father. No family of money-thin unfortunates ever went away hungry from Pop Worley's general store—particularly if there were any little kids in need. That was Pop Worley for you—the best of the best!

"It was nighttime, closing-up time. Pop was alone, busy at the cash drawer, totaling up. Then this drifter, a bandanna across his face, charged in out of the night waving a gun. And Pop, while he would cheerfully give the shirt off his back to anyone he thought needed it more than he did himself, was too salty to stand still while being robbed at gunpoint. In consequence, he went for his own gun. He never got there. The thieving rat in front of him shot him down, then set about scooping up the money in the cash drawer.

"Pop didn't last very long after that, but he did live long enough to tell of getting a good look at the hand that was scooping up the cash. It was a left hand—a left hand with only four fingers on it. The middle finger was missing. Now, would that mean anything to anybody here?"

At first mention of the town of Meridian, Hube Marion had stiffened, and the quick glance he threw at Jud Hilliard was charged with a banked ferocity. The room had gone dead-still and remained so until Hilliard spoke again, the words falling chill and ominous across a straining quiet.

"Because I'm here to collect for Pop Worley!"

This bleak pronouncement set Hube Marion off. He came away from the bar in a whirling rush, his right hand streaking for the gun at his hip, the desperate move of a thoroughly desperate renegade. It did him no good, for he was behind in the all-important moment of truth. And the blasting roar that shook the room was the voice of the gun Jud Hilliard drew and used with savage, deadly purpose. The result bore out that purpose. The lethal slug that smashed into Hube Marion knocked him down and left him huddled on the floor.

Through the shadow of a bitter regret over the necessity of such things as this, Jud Hilliard laid out both a cold glance and some measured words for the other occupants of the place.

"Any questions?"

There were none. From behind the bar Buck Saddler stood wordless, staring across at the figure on the floor. Nile Starkey, licking loose and nervous lips, leaned heavily against the bar, as though needing support.

"I traveled a long, long way to catch up with a four-fingered rat," Jud Hilliard said, "and I just did!"

He turned back to the door, pausing there to lay out a final word. "No need any of you aiming to send word of this out to Marion headquarters. I'm riding out there myself to report it!"

Behind him, he left a room that seemed enormously still after being rocked with the heavy voice of a deadly gun. Trying to pour a hefty jolt of whiskey for himself, Buck Saddler fumbled badly, spilling liquor on the bar. He tried to curse himself back to steadiness, but he spilled even more when he aimed at Nile Starkey's glass.

"He did it!" he managed to mumble. "Just like that, he did it!"

"Yeah," agreed Nile Starkey heavily. "Just like that!"

CHAPTER
9

THE Marion ranch house lay shaded and quiet when Jud Hilliard rode up to it. A little pinto pony standing at the tie rail was evidence of another recent arrival.

"Cody!" Hilliard murmured to himself. "I wonder how much she's told?"

He put big Red in beside the pinto and stepped down. The ranch-house door opened, and Garr Marion showed, tossing a beckoning hand.

"Jud! Come on in, man—come on in. You're just in time to hear the best of news concerning Parker. Cody's giving the word to Father right now. Yeah, come on in!"

Pausing at the door, Hilliard laid out sober words. "Got something to report myself, Garr. It's why I'm here."

Garr stared. "Man, that has a strange sound. What is it?"

"Best I tell it direct to your father. You can listen in, and I'm hoping you'll reserve judgment until you've heard all of it."

Caleb Marion occupied his usual chair before the hearth in the big, beamed room. Cody stood beside her father, an arm resting across his shoulders. The iron-faced old soldier was smiling as he looked at Hilliard and growled welcome.

"Glad to see you again, friend—and happy over a better feeling in the air than when last you faced me. This girl of mine brings the best of news concerning my youngest son—the given word of Dr. Craig that Parker is well along the way to becoming a whole man again. Now we can all rejoice!"

"Over that, sir, I gladly join you," Hilliard said quietly. "But I'm here to report something at the other extreme. It has to do with your nephew, Hube Marion. And I know you'd want me to tell it straight out. Back in town at Buck Saddler's Gilt Edge bar, I settled a deep and long-standing debt with Hube Marion. It was for that express purpose I came into this hill country in the first place, hoping to catch up with a four-fingered thief and murderer!" Hilliard squared his shoulders as he added the final somber words. "That thief and murderer was Hube Marion. When I put the facts in front of him, he went for his gun. He didn't get there!"

For a long breath or two a suspended, overall silence held. Then an eruptive growl rumbled in Caleb Marion's throat, which Garr echoed in only slightly lesser tone. The old man surged forward as though about to rear to his feet despite his physical infirmity. But Cody was quick to hold him back while laying out a flat statement of her own.

"Dad, Garr—be sensible—both of you! And listen, I've more to report about Parker. Last night while Dr. Craig was resting, I sat with Parker, keeping watch. And Parker spoke to me, telling about the shooting that took place when he happened to meet up with the Dorcass brothers and Hube, who was riding with them. They were driving a small gather of Marion cattle. It was Duff Dorcass who shot Parker's horse, and Parker shot back, believing he hit Duff Dorcass. And then it was Hube—his own cousin—who shot Parker. Dad, you and Garr should think about that. All we Marions should think about it and what it could have led to. And then thank Jud Hilliard, which I certainly do!"

Her head was up and her eyes misty with tears as she looked at Hilliard. He tipped his head. "I salute both wisdom and courage!" He turned to

Garr. "There's a considerable story behind this, if you'd care to listen. Something that could make for a better, all-around understanding."

In their own right both he and Garr were strong men as they now faced each other, two men brought together through circumstance to meet in a new, but real, friendship. Garr nodded. "Go ahead, tell it!"

Which Hilliard did, from its very start back in the distant town of Meridian. Leaning far forward, Caleb Marion did not miss a single word. When Hilliard finished, the old man eased back, nodding and growling his troubled thoughts. "As I recall now, he was away at that time and we wondered about it. Now we know where and why."

Silent for a time, Caleb Marion stared straight ahead, his face tight with feeling. He sighed deeply before speaking again.

"So he turned out renegade, did he—just plain damn renegade. It should be no real surprise. Over the years there were several times I had cause to wonder about Hube Marion and whether he was a sound and worthwhile man. But I was too blind with misplaced pride to admit that he wasn't and to take proper steps. So now I must live with my shame."

Quickly Cody's arms were around him, hugging his grizzled head. "Not with shame, Father—just with truth!"

Clearing a gruff throat, Garr moved across the room, pausing in front of Jud Hilliard, hand outstretched.

Their hands met, then Garr turned to his father. "I'll go into town after him. The rest of this is strictly up to the Marion family."

"Just so." Caleb Marion nodded. "Up to us, strictly!"

When Hilliard turned to leave, Cody followed him to the door, then out to the tie rail where big Red nuzzled her shoulder and nickered softly as she reached up to pet him. She spoke with a pensive hesitancy.

"And—and what now, Jud Hilliard, since you've fulfilled your vow of vengeance? Where—where away now?"

Hilliard smiled down at her. "For the present, no farther than town. Because Red and me, both of us have found some mighty good friends in these hills, people it would never be easy to ride away from"

Hilliard mounted Red and reined him in the direction of town.

Cody watched him drop down the slope, splash through the creek, and move across the meadow into the timber. There was warm color tinting her cheeks, and her glance held a soft steadiness.

In town, Hilliard hauled up at the livery stable and found Skeeter Dahl squirming with curiosity.

"Man—oh, man!" Skeeter sputtered. "You sure

got this town stirred up and ready to run. I'm about ready to take off myself, just like Nile Starkey already has. Which I can't figger. What you got against him?"

The hint of a renewed ease that had begun to form in Jud Hilliard's expression became a wondering scowl. "Nothing in particular outside a touch of personal dislike. Certainly not enough of that to really mean anything."

"Starkey must have figgered differently," vowed Skeeter, "for he sure enough has hauled foot. This sure has Cluny Grimes plenty upset and blaming you, because Starkey has been his star boarder. For that matter it's costing me some, too, as Starkey stalled his horse regular with me. Yes, sir—mister, when you gunned Hube Marion, you sure raised hell in big chunks. And right now I can't figger why the rest of the Marions ain't on your trail plenty!"

Gravely thoughtful, Hilliard shrugged. "Things you don't know, Skeeter. Things a lot of people don't know. So don't be guessing wild about anything, as you could be way wrong. There's plenty of quality in certain members of the Marion family, with only Hube proving badly off strain. Maybe the good ones feel they're well rid of him and have the courage and honesty to say so."

Skeeter considered for a moment before nodding. "Sounds reasonable enough," he admitted. Skeeter reached for Red's rein. "Come on, big feller—that box stall is ready and waitin' for you."

Heading for the hotel, Jud Hilliard moved a little slowly, feeling a drained weariness that was more emotional than physical. As he turned in at the hotel door Cluny Grimes was there to face him, the frightened, rabbitlike expression more pronounced than ever before.

Noticing this reaction, Hilliard knew a touch of grim amusement and spoke it. "I understand that certain conditions I've lately moved through have, for some reason I fail to understand, cost you a regular tenant, Cluny. I'm sorry about that. Now, if it is all right with you, I'll hole up for a time in my room."

Cluny gulped, then bleated, "Of course, of course. You're always welcome here."

Climbing the stairs to his room, Hilliard wondered about that and told himself so soberly. "You're a marked man in these parts from now on. You've solved one problem, but you have more facing you."

Shucking his boots and gun, he sprawled on his bed, seeking ease there, but it was an ease slow in coming. His thoughts went all the way back to a roundup camp in the sagebrush country where a kindly old black man had fed him and told him flat out that vengeance business was not always good business. Maybe Old Zeke had spoken with wise prophecy. Hilliard was still playing with that thought when he dozed off.

In her eating house, Hester Loring sat up at the counter with a cup of coffee before her. Beyond the counter, old Ab Roblin was busy putting a bowl of biscuit dough together. While he worked, Ab sketched out the facts of the last few days as he knew them.

"This fellow Hilliard—this newcomer to our town—he sure has everybody wondering and jumping. Tough one, that fellow!"

Outside, a buckboard and team with a lone occupant pulled in at the hitch rail. The lone occupant was Caleb Marion. Using his crutch expertly, he lowered himself from the rig, looked up and down the street, his shaggy head swinging truculently. Then he clumped to the door, pushed it open, and came in. Ab Roblin exclaimed his wonder and stood openmouthed. Hester Loring spun around and faced Caleb Marion, her head high, her shoulders combatively straight.

"This," she said coldly, "I never expected to see. You—Caleb Marion—in this house. There is something you wanted—someone you wanted to see?"

"Yes," rumbled the old soldier, "someone I wanted to see. You!" He took off his hat. "Miss Loring, you are looking at a very humble man. An old fool, if that would be more fitting, but still a humble one. I am here to apologize for all the stupid past, the product of what I used to call pride, thinking such pride important. It wasn't. And there is none of it left. I would thank you for all you've done for the Marion family—in particular caring for my son, Parker. And while I don't deserve any, I'd like to ask for a little forgiveness for me."

The combative tilt in her shoulders lessened along with the chill in her glance. This old man was being very contrite. She showed him a warming smile. "What's past," she said quietly, "is past. And I'm very happy that your son Parker is definitely out of the woods and on a safe way back."

"Yes." Caleb Marion nodded. "Thanks to you—and others." He looked around. "There was a little fellow...a lad?"

"Having his afternoon nap."

"Someday," Caleb Marion said, "I would like to know that lad better." He turned to the door. "Thank you again and again. Through the years ahead I'll always be thanking you."

He spun on his crutch and stumped out.

Openmouthed, then mumbling, Ab Roblin stared after him. "Now, there was something I never expected to see or hear. An ornery old blister like him near down on his knees to anyone, man or woman!"

Hester Loring's smile was small and warm. "For years I've felt I hated him and that I always would. Now I find that I don't. You know, Ab—it took a lot of character and courage to come in here and admit all that he did. A lesser man wouldn't have been equal to it."

Ab Roblin nodded agreement. "It's like what Skeeter Dahl's been saying. When that new feller Hilliard gunned down Hube Marion, he sure shook things up in these parts!"

The Logan Canyon road leading to the distant town of Keystone was narrow and twisting, in one spot cutting between two craggy, barren rock faces. On the crest of one of these Elgie Dorcass crouched. He was ragged, dirty and unkempt, gaunt, and looking half starved. He had a rifle laid out beside him and had been waiting with an almost wild animal patience for a quarry he was certain would be passing this way. Now that quarry was before him—a rider constantly urging his horse to a faster gait. Elgie brought his rifle to his shoulder and laid out a thin, high-pitched challenge.

"Haul up, Starkey—haul up! You can stop right there!"

Riding slightly hunched, shoulders sagging, Nile Starkey reined in abruptly, head swinging, startled glance seeking and finding and stirring gusty exclamation.

"Elgie—Elgie Dorcass! What is this, man—what is this?"

"Somethin' I aim to settle right here and now,"

Elgie told him tightly. "After what happened to Hube Marion I figgered you'd be headin' out before you met up with somethin' of the same. And I figgered right, didn't I? Well, you don't pull a run-out that easy—not much you don't!"

Nile Starkey licked nervous lips, a betraying habit of his when the chips were down and he wasn't sure which way the next card would fall. His answering words now were gusty and uneven.

"Hell, man—there's no need of anything like this. There's no quarrel between you and me. What happened with Hube Marion and that fellow Hilliard concerned just the two of them, and from the way Hilliard talked, he'd been on Hube's trail for a long time and across a big run of country for something strictly between the two of them. And nothing for us to fuss about."

"But Hube's dead now," Elgie droned. "And old Duff is dead, which is the main thing that's between you and me. Because you and Hube talked Duff and me into this thing. You made it sound good and reasonable, so we listened and got led into it. All we had to do was help move a little jag of Marion beef over on to Sam Wade's range. Make it look like Sam had done it and then for us to talk it up that way, so's to get the old Marion–Wade feud goin' again."

Elgie paused, shifting his position a little, his rifle always couched and ready. "Yeah," he went on, "the idea was to get the old Marion–Wade feud stirred up and goin' again, and when both sides were weakened down, we'd move in and take over everything. It was big bait, Starkey— real big bait for fellers like Duff and me, and we went for it. We should have known better, of course. But we'd never amounted to much, never owned much of anything, either. And with Hube Marion all set to go against his own kin—well, Duff and me were fooled complete."

Again Elgie shifted slightly before laying out more harsh words. "But you were the one with the real slick talk, Starkey—and more and more it shapes up to me that the whole thing was mainly your idea. And you talked old Duff and me into it. But like I say, both Hube and Duff are dead now, while I'm on the dodge and it's plain you're aimin' to skin out. But you ain't about to make it, Starkey—not much you ain't! No sir, mister—you ain't about to make it!"

From the very beginning of this face-off, from the moment of Elgie's first bleak call and challenge, Nile Starkey had known full well that this was it! That gaunt, ragged, dirty figure crouched atop the rock face was nemesis—retribution! And the issue was certain and deadly.

A thread of cold terror whipped through Nile Starkey. He had a gun, a snub-barreled weapon of heavy caliber that was a sagging weight in his coat pocket. But how could he get hold of it in time to do any good?

Maybe if he just kept talking, Elgie would ease up on that watchful, fixed alertness and enable him to maneuver a break. So ran Starkey's desperate thoughts. It was his only chance, his only out, so he took it with words that fell jocular and careless.

"Hell, Elgie—it just don't make sense for you and me to be arguing like this. Let's calm down, have a smoke, and figure out a new idea that would be good for both of us!"

Speaking, Starkey dropped a hand into his pocket as though reaching for his smoking gear. He gripped the gun, hauled it out, and tried to lift it into line. The move was fast and desperate, but futile, as Elgie's rifle blasted a hard, snarling report. A massive blow hammered into Nile Starkey's chest, driving him back against the cantle of his saddle where he wavered for a short breath of time while all the substance of life drained out of him. Then he toppled and went headlong into the road's thin dust, never knowing the impact as the earth took him. Snorting, his startled horse swung wide.

While jacking a fresh cartridge into the reeking chamber of his rifle, Elgie Dorcass turned his head to put a long, fixed stare back across the misted crest of timbered hills, his murmured words lost in the great, hanging silence.

"That one was special for you, Duff!"

* * *

156

For the second time in the space of a few hours, Garr Marion rode into the town of Willow Creek. The first time was by spring wagon and team to haul away the blanket-wrapped body of the Marion clan's one proven renegade. Throughout this somber chore Garr's face had been locked in a bleak, grim coldness. On his second visit, however, he came by saddle, and as he swung up at the hitch rail of Hester Loring's eating house, there was eagerness in his stride as he stepped down and went in.

At first no one was in sight, but when the rear door of the room opened, it was Hester Loring and her youngster, Terry, who showed. The lad raced quickly around the end of the counter to climb on the stool beside Garr, whose ready arm aided and steadied the little fellow. For a moment of grave silence Hester Loring eyed the pair of them, but her words soft and wondering.

"Never saw him act so before. Most generally, with strangers, he's shy."

"Terry and me, we're not strangers," returned Garr cheerfully. "Instead the best of friends." He smiled down at the boy. "How about that, partner?"

The youngster wriggled his agreement.

"And here is something more," Garr went on. "I'm under orders from headquarters to bring Terry out there. And not wanting to separate the boy from his mother, she, of course, will have to come along with us."

Some heat still lingered in the big cooking range, and a coffeepot was gurgling gently. Hester Loring filled two cups from this, put them on the counter, and circled to come up on the other side of Terry, speaking quietly.

"Now that is somewhat sudden, as well as being something I must do considerable thinking on."

"Don't see why," Garr countered, looking at her very steadily. "You've long known how I feel about you."

Warm color touched her cheeks as she met and held his glance. "There—there's Terry you know, Garr."

"Just so." Garr nodded. "Which only makes my feelings stronger. He's part of the bargain—a mighty welcome part."

Now an almost girlish shyness held her, and her words were unsteady. "I—I must tell you about him. He is not my natural son. His real mother was my sister. His father was killed in a freighting accident, and sister Nell did not last long after that. So Terry, still in swaddling clothes, became mine. And feeling that every little boy should have someone he could call 'Mother,' I've played that part ever since. And gloried in it. Someday, perhaps, when he is old enough to understand about such things, I may tell him the truth."

Again Garr looked at her, and what she saw in

his eyes put a mist of tears in her own. Garr captured her hand, and his words fell huskily.

"Wonderful, wonderful woman! And now, will you come along with Terry and me...?"

Her answer was in the warm pressure of her fingers.

CHAPTER
10

STILL clinging to the solitude of his hotel room and nagged by a restlessness that kept him prowling back and forth like something caged, Jud Hilliard labored at figuring some sort of reasonably solid future for himself and his affairs. Just what, he pondered, lay ahead for him?

At this moment the town of Meridian was a far-distant world that was becoming more distant with every passing day. The thought of ever returning there was less and less appealing.

In Meridian lay only the store and the memories tied to it. And memories, he had found, under the inexorable erosion of time, could not sustain any man forever. If Pop Morley were alive and there, things could appear different. But Pop was gone and the odyssey of vengeance that paid off for the old fellow's brutal death had been fulfilled in a few gun-reeking moments right across the street yonder in Buck Saddler's Gilt Edge bar.

So much for the past! Hilliard mused bleakly. But what about the future?

In Meridian the banker, Jonathan Peabody, who had been one of Pop Worley's oldest and best friends, could be counted on to dispose of the store and other holdings for the best possible values and stood ready to forward the funds on written request. Just what the total might be could only be guessed at, though perhaps enough to offer some chance at a new start with cattle in some likely spot in these hills.

Hilliard was savoring that thought when echoing up from the street through the room's open window came the shuffle of tired equine hoofs and the creak of iron stage wheels being braked to a halt. Moving over to the window, Hilliard looked down at a street where evening's first early shades were beginning to gather. Down there old Gil Benton had brought the Keystone stage to a halt and was in the act of tossing a thin mail sack down to Cluny Grimes, who stood waiting on the hotel porch. The stage driver's words carried clearly up to Hilliard.

"Nothin' much in that sack, Cluny. But I got a mite of other news that could stir up the folks. There's a dead man layin' 'longside the road back in the canyon narrows. It's that feller Starkey, the cattle buyer whose been in these parts so considerable of late. He'd been shot. I'd'a brought him in with me, only at my age I ain't up to rasslin' no dead man around by myself. So you better cut over to the Gilt Edge and tell Buck Saddler about it. Buck'll likely know what to do."

Cluny Grimes began to stutter. "G-G-Gil, you realize what you're saying? That Mister Starkey's been shot and is layin' back in the canyon...dead! You sure you ain't drunk and just imaginin' things?"

"I ain't imaginin' nothin'," retorted the stage driver bluntly. "And I ain't drunk, neither—as I ain't had a drink all day. But I sure could stand a big one about now, seein' I'm no way used to findin' dead men along the road. So you get on over and tell Buck about it."

Stirring his team to movement, old Gil headed on along to Skeeter Dahl's livery stable and corrals.

Catching up his hat, Jud Hilliard stopped downstairs, meeting Cluny Grimes along the way. Cluny's pop eyes were even more protuberant than usual as he stared at Hilliard almost accusingly.

"From the day you first showed in these hills damn world's been comin' apart," he bleated. "You know what Gil Benton just told me? Gil said—"

"I know what he said," Hilliard cut in. "I was listening at my window, and I want to talk to Benton. Maybe he left out something."

Cluny was almost whimpering. "Poor Mister Starkey! He was such a generous man. Always paid his room bill on time. Who would have wanted to kill him? And why?"

"That," Hilliard said briefly, "is the point that interests me—the why of it."

At the stable, while he and Skeeter Dahl were unhooking the stage team, Gil Benton was repeating his story to Skeeter, who was all ears and openmouthed. When Hilliard approached, Skeeter turned to him. "You know what Gil found along the canyon road?"

"I know," Hilliard said. "I heard him give the word to Cluny Grimes. And I've a question to ask." He turned to the stage driver. "Old timer, did you see anybody else along the way besides the dead man you found?"

Gil Benton nodded. "Yeah, there was a feller. Passed him clear back at the mouth of the canyon. He was movin' right along, like in a hurry to get somewhere."

"Ever see him before?"

Again Gil Benton nodded. "A time or two, here about town. Him and his brother—they made a pair, always together. Heard their name once but can't recall it easy. Kind of a funny name."

"Such as Dorcass, maybe?" Hilliard suggested.

For a third time the old stage driver bobbed a grizzled head. "That's it!"

"Was he packing a gun?"

"Yeah. Had a rifle slung under his leg."

Not missing a word, Skeeter Dahl turned to Jud Hilliard. "More or less paints a picture, wouldn't you say, friend?"

"Just so," Hilliard agreed. "But not an easy one to read. Has a lot of whys and wherefores in it."

"Wonder what Cluny Grimes thinks," Skeeter hazarded to say.

Hilliard's answer was brief and dry. "When I left him, he was moaning and wringing his hands. I had the feeling that his concern was not so much that Nile Starkey was dead as it was that he'd been robbed of a tenant who—as Cluny himself put it—always paid his room rent on time."

A shadow of wry amusement touched Skeeter's lips. "Now, that's Cluny for you—always with his eye out for the dollar. And, friend, this shapes up as a chore for some of us. Not a pleasant chore but one that in all human decency has to be done. I'll hook a team to a wagon." He looked at Jud Hilliard meaningfully. "A hand, maybe?"

"Of course," Hilliard agreed quietly. "I never cared for the man, but at a time like this such feeling doesn't count."

They found Nile Starkey where the stage driver said they would. At the canyon's rock-ribbed narrows. Skeeter had his look around. "A perfect spot to lay out if you were set to gulch somebody."

"Just so," Hilliard agreed. "Particularly if you had it figured that a certain person would, sooner or later, be passing this way. All of which raises another damn question to wonder over: Why? I'll prowl a little."

He ended up atop the rock shoulder to pick up a recently fired rifle shell. He tossed the empty down. "Right from here, Skeeter."

"A rough world," observed Skeeter somberly. "A damn rough world. Man has to hold a real grip on himself to keep from spookin'!"

When they got back to town, a sober-faced Garr Marion waited at the stable door. He'd already heard the stage driver's story, so he showed no great surprise when Hilliard and Skeeter came rolling in with their grim burden.

"Was hoping to meet up with you," he told Hilliard. "Just came from the Clement ranch where I'd been to see for myself how Parker was making out."

"And the report?"

"Couldn't be better," Garr assured. "Park is coming along so well, everybody is set to cheer. But what has me fighting my head is the experience Doc Craig went through the other night. Damnedest story I ever heard. And it could tell us something about the why of this very thing."

Before speaking, Garr glanced at the huddled figure of Nile Starkey in Skeeter's wagon. "But first I'll help you get him out of sight and under cover."

Later, backs to the stable wall, they squatted on their heels in the now slanting sunshine while seeking the solace of pipe and cigarette.

"This," Garr said, "is what happened to Doc Craig out at the Clement ranch. He'd gone outside for a quiet smoke under the stars. Out of the dark came this fellow to stick a gun in Doc's ribs and march him up and into the edge of the timber, telling him he was needed to give medical aid to somebody. That somebody was laid out, wrapped in a blanket. Somebody named Duff—that's what the fellow with the gun kept calling him. Yeah, Duff—good old Duff.

"Doc said the moment he laid hands on the fellow in the blanket, he knew the man was most thoroughly dead and beyond any kind of medical help. When he stated that fact, the one with the gun turned savage—almost a little crazy—so much so that Doc thought the threatening gun might be turned on him. But finally he was allowed to return to the ranch house, which he was damned glad to do. Doc said somebody else might make sense out of the affair, though he couldn't figure it personally. What's your thought, Jud?"

"The Dorcass brothers, of course. Duff the dead one; Elgie the one with the gun. And from all that has happened today it must have been Elgie who laid out at the canyon narrows to gulch Nile Starkey. Which raises the big question of why he should have done this, because Starkey didn't kill Duff Dorcass. According to what Parker told his sister, Cody, he was the one who got lead into Duff. That points up more and more the reason Elgie Dorcass laid out to get Starkey—he figured some kind of double cross was in the wind and that Starkey was about to weasel out of a deal that had turned sour."

Garr nodded gravely. "You're making sense. So keep on. I'm all ears."

Jud Hilliard's glance ranged the empty street, but he was seeing only what lay behind his mind's eye. "I've been doing considerable thinking on the whole setup, Garr. Let's go back to the day Park met up with the Dorcass brothers and his own cousin, Hube, hazing the Marion cattle. Why were they driving them onto Sam Wade's range?"

Hilliard's pipe had begun to fry, and he paused to knock the dottle from it against a boot heel.

"Yeah, the why of it," he went on. "It had to be an attempt to stir up the old feud between Caleb Marion and Sam Wade. But who stood to benefit from another feud? Could it have been Starkey, sitting in the background and posing as a cattle buyer? As such, he was in a perfect position to find a market for the Marion and Wade cattle rustled while Caleb Marion and Sam Wade were tied up in a renewal of the old trouble."

Again Hilliard paused, adding and subtracting the ominous possibilities tracking through his mind. He shook a troubled head, exclaiming, "Oh, hell, Garr—I admit I'm supposing and guessing at a lot of things. Considering that fellow Nile Starkey, I must admit I've had no use for him from the moment I first laid eyes on him. Call it instinct if you want. But whatever, that's the way it was and is. And judging from the stand you took the other morning at breakfast, backing old Ab Roblin's hand all the way, Nile Starkey must have rubbed against the grain with you too. This brings us to the fact that Elgie Dorcass laid out for a chance to gun Starkey down."

"Just so," Garr agreed. "More and more I begin to get the drift of your thinking and reasoning. Because Elgie wouldn't've gunned Starkey just for the hell of it, would he?"

Hilliard shook his head. "No, he wouldn't. I see Elgie feeling that he and Duff had been used and double-crossed in some kind of deal that had turned sour and that Starkey was trying to sneak out of, a move Elgie coppered with a .30-30 slug."

Garr pushed to his feet, took a deep breath, stretched his arms, and spoke with quiet conviction. "You know, Jud Hilliard, in one way or another you've been a mighty good person for this spread of country and all of its affairs. I'm hoping you intend to stay on with us. Now, guess I'd best be heading for home."

After Garr rode away, the street lay empty again. The day was well along, and hunger was stirring in Hilliard, sending him to his room to wash up before heading for the Hester's eating house where he found Ab Roblin alone. Ab eyed Hilliard soberly.

"High time somebody showed up," he said, "what with Miss Hester and Terry the little fellow visiting at Marion headquarters, things in this damn town are plenty lonely."

"Been a long day, Ab—with many things happening," Hilliard returned. "And with some of those things, all for the better with some mighty fine people both you and I think a lot of."

Ab bobbed a grizzled head. "Just so, just so! Mebbe you and me should celebrate a little. I got a good steak set aside for you, and for both of us, how about a nip of something a mite stronger than coffee?"

Grinning, Ab reached under the counter and

came up with a couple of glasses and a bottle. "Some of Buck Saddler's prime Kentucky bourbon," he said, pouring.

Hilliard lifted his glass. "To the future and all-time happiness of a pair of great people, Ab. To Garr Marion and Hester Loring!"

"You bet!" Ab exclaimed. "We sure will drink to that!"

The steak, perfectly cooked, along with hot biscuits and coffee, sent Hilliard away replete.

Dusk had settled in across this high mountain world. The early stars were glinting in a darkening sky, which let down a breath of chill that made Hilliard hunch his shoulders and quicken his steps as he sought the sanctuary of his hotel room, there to renew his plans for the future.

After breakfast tomorrow, he decided, he and Red would do some traveling, searching these hills for a spot where he might begin building a headquarters of his own.

In the first flare of morning's searching sunshine Skeeter Dahl was taking his ease beside the stable door. He watched Jud Hilliard come briskly along from the Hester's eating house.

"You," Skeeter observed smugly, "act like you're figgering on goin' somewhere."

"Just so," Hilliard told him. "Red and me, we're going to move around a little, get some exercise while we look over the country."

Skeeter showed a small, sly grin. "Red ain't here. He's already out, gettin' his exercise."

Hilliard came sharply around. "What's that, what's that? Red's not here? What're you talking about? Nobody rides that horse without my permission. Nobody!"

Skeeter's grin broadened. "Me, I never argue with a lady. Neither does Red. From the way he nickered and nosed her shoulder he was plumb tickled to see her. And that little pinto bronc seems near lost in Red's big box stall."

The harshness in Hilliard's words and manner vanished. "So that's it, eh? The lady? Cody Marion, of course?"

Skeeter's grin became a satisfied chuckle. "She looked like a little kid up on that big red rascal. Ain't too mad, are you?"

It was Hilliard's turn to grin. "I'm like you, Skeeter. I never argue with a lady." He got out his pipe, packed and lit it. "Move over and let me have some of that sunshine. Not a thing to do but wait for her to get back."

"Just so," Skeeter agreed. "Said she wanted to go out to the Clement ranch to check on Parker's condition. And with big Red plumb anxious to do some fast travelin', she shouldn't be too long."

Nor was she, for presently the rumble of nearing hoofs could be heard, and the big red horse stormed into town and pulled up at the stable door. Cody Marion looked down at Hilliard a little diffidently. "I—I hope you won't be too angry at me. But I wanted the latest about Parker. And I knew how Red loves to run."

She leaned forward and patted a sleek, powerful, red shoulder. "I—I'm sorry if you feel I had no—no right. But I knew this big beautiful fellow wouldn't mind."

"I'd disown him if he did," Hilliard declared. "And what did you find out about Park?"

"Mainly that it was no place for me. When I left, Sally Wade was sitting by Park's bed and they were holding hands. So, as a mere sister, I was of no importance at all. And now, Jud Hilliard, I return your horse to you." She started to swing from the saddle, but Hilliard, moving closer swiftly, reached up.

"Long way down for a small, would-be horse stealer. I'd better help!"

For a full moment she hesitated, searching his glance and reading the gentle, unmistakable message it carried. She matched it with a sweet glance of her own and slid down into the waiting circle of his arms.